# camp CONFIDENTIAL

## Second Summer

Best (Boy)friend Forever

**Visit us at www.abdopublishing.com**

Reinforced library bound edition published in 2009 by Spotlight, a division of ABDO Group, 8000 West 78th Street, Edina, Minnesota 55439. This library bound edition is published by arrangement with Grosset & Dunlap, a member of Penguin Group (USA) Inc.

Front cover image © Teenage Living/Image100.Ltd. /Veer Incorporated. Cover background image © Mayang Murni Adnin, 2001-2005, www.mayang.com/textures. Text copyright © 2006 by Grosset & Dunlap. All rights reserved. Published by Grosset & Dunlap, a division of Penguin Young Readers Group, 345 Hudson Street, New York, NY 10014. GROSSET & DUNLAP is a trademark of Penguin Group (USA) Inc.

**Library of Congress Cataloging-in-Publication Data**
This title was previously cataloged with the following information:
Morgan, Melissa J.
    Best (boy)friend forever / by Melissa J. Morgan.
    p. cm. -- (Camp Confidential ; 9)
    Summary: During her third year at Camp Lakeview, resident tomboy Priya finds that being best friends with a boy has some drawbacks now that they are both growing up.
    [1. Camps--Fiction. 2. Best friends--Fiction. 3. Friendships--Fiction. 4. Interpersonal relations--Fiction.] I. Title. II. Series.
PZ7.M82545 Be 2006
[Fic]--dc22                                          2006002439

ISBN 0-448-44325-2 (paperback)
ISBN: 978-1-59961-504-2 (reinforced library bound edition)

All Spotlight books have reinforced library binding
and are manufactured in the United States of America.

# camp CONFIDENTIAL

## Second Summer

## Best (Boy)friend Forever

by Melissa J. Morgan

Grosset & Dunlap

# chapter ONE

Hey, Sam-bone!

Sorry I haven't written more, li'l bro. But you know how much I hate to sit still. And there's always so much to do at Camp Lakeview. B-ball. Swimming in the lake. Soccer. Moonlight hikes. And some pretty great pranks have been played already this year. The most extreme ones since Jordan and I started coming here. Wow, I can hardly believe it's our third summer. (Jordan says hi and says to go next door and scratch Cougar's belly for him, because his parents always forget how much Cougar loves belly scratchies.)

A couple days ago, I had this tree-climbing contest with Jordan, and I almost fell. Don't tell Mom! I won, so it's all good. Except the next day, Jordan beat me in this game we invented. Bike-broom polo. We'll teach it to you when we get home. You'll go ape over it.

With the tree and the polo included, that makes the overall score for the summer—Priya 43—Jordan 41. I so rule! Except that, okay, Jordan has been ahead of me a couple times in this summer's private Who's-the-Most-Extreme Challenge. We've always managed to keep it a secret from the counselors in the past, but this year there have been a couple-few visits to the nurse. There was even some hoo-ha about how I could have broken a bone after someone not-cool saw me in the tree. If I had broken one, you know what that would have meant? I'd be even with you and Jordan in bone breaking. (And Mom would say stupidity!) Because, as you know, I've had two broken bones in my almost twelve years on the planet, plus that thing that time with my tooth. What's that Dad says? The thrill of victory, the agony of defeat? I still say the thrill was worth the agony of the teeth. 'Cause I did conquer that empty swimming pool with my skateboard. You know it.

How're you? How's the all-star team? Getting to play at D-land, that so rocks. I miss you, but with my best friend here, do I really need my annoying little brother around? (Just kidding. Jordan's my BBFF. That's boy best friend forever, in case you don't know. But you're my BBF. Best brother forever. Duh.)

I can't wait until Friday. That's when the whole 4th Division is heading off for our long weekend—5 days!!!—in Washington, D.C. There are a bunch of different activities to pick from, with pairs of counselors chaperoning each one. Jordan and I have already made a zillion plans. We're definitely going to do this thing called Sites on Bikes. That's where you bike around all the monuments. (Do you think it's possible to scale the Washington Monument? Because how much insane fun would it be to rappel down that thing? Just kidding. Mostly. I mean it would be fun, but even I'm not that deranged.) And we're going to spend one whole day in the National Air and Space Museum. Of course. Two astro-nuts like us couldn't miss that. There's also this dance-cruise thing on the Potomac River the last night that everyone has to go to. I'm not so into that. But Jordan and I will find some way to make it fun.

Gotta go. Time for swimming.

Bye!

Your favorite (and, okay, only) sister,

Priya

▲ ▲ ▲

Priya Shah swam toward the big wooden raft out in the lake part of Camp Lakeview. She loved to lie on it until she started to get just a little dry. Then dive into the cold blue-green water. Then dry. Then dive. Then dry. Then—

Get hauled straight to the bottom!

Something had her by the foot and was dragging her down, down, down. Make that some*one!* Jordan played this trick on her at least once during every swimming session. She did a fast flip-twist-roll, the combo that she always used to get free from Jordan's power grip, and shot up to the surface like a bubble in a can of Coke.

Jordan popped up next to her about a second later. "You need some new routines," Priya told him.

"I'm thinkin' we need more B.T.L.," Jordan said.

If you didn't know Jordan, you might think he was saying he wanted more bacon, tomato, and lettuce sandwiches. But Priya knew Jordan and the way Jordan's brain worked. To Jordan, B.T.L. could only mean one thing. The Beyond the Limits section of the National Air and Space Museum.

"We already calculated how much time we can

spend at every exhibit we want to see," Priya reminded him as they treaded water across from each other. They'd been planning the museum part of the D.C. trip almost from the moment Dr. Steve announced it.

"I know. But B.T.L. has the full-size space shuttle cockpit simulator. I need more minutes with that," Jordan told her.

"Fine. Just don't take them away from the Clementine. It—"

"I know, I know," Jordan interrupted. "The lunar exploration vehicle that went from drawing board to space in two years." Jordan knew how her brain worked, too. "But, Priya," he continued. "I'm tellin' you, that doesn't mean that you can make one in your garage."

Priya splashed him with one hand, using the other one to keep treading water. "Can I just say—duh?"

"I know how you think," Jordan insisted. "Some day I'll come over and it will be like that scene in *E.T.* You'll have a fork and a phone and a bunch of other garbage and you'll be trying to put yourself in orbit."

Priya lowered her mouth into the water and shot a stream at him. "The Clementine was unmanned."

"Fish poop in that water, you know," Jordan informed her.

"So we're both swimming in fish poop," Priya answered.

Jordan stared at her for a second, a disgusted expression crawling over his face. Then he cracked up.

"I see you and the boyfriend found a new place

for a private conversation," Gaby commented as the 4C girls headed back to their bunk after swimming.

Priya rolled her eyes. She knew Gaby just called Jordan her boyfriend because Gaby knew that it drove her bonkers. But she couldn't stop herself from exclaiming, "For probably the five hundredth time, Jordan is my friend. Period. Friend. Nothing before it. Friend. Friend. Got it, Gaby?"

Gaby raised her eyebrows. "Okay. You and that boy who is your friend seemed to have an awful lot to talk about today. And it didn't seem like you wanted anyone else listening in, since you were talking while treading water away from everybody."

"Yeah, that's why you two climbed to the top of that tree the other day, right?" Grace teased. "So you'd have privacy to tell each other how much you loooove each other."

"Don't be stupid," Priya said, but she smiled. At least Grace was just being goofy. Not trying to start trouble, which was what Gaby seemed to live for.

"It's not stupid. Trees are the classic place for romance." Brynn slapped her hands over her heart, her green eyes bright with laughter.

"What are you talking about?" Alex, the bunk's own Mia Hamm, asked, kicking a soccer ball along the trail in front of her.

Brynn smiled. "Haven't you ever heard that rhyme about being in a tree? K-I—"

"S-S-I-N-G!" everyone finished with her.

"We were C-L-I-M-B-I-N-G," Priya told them.

"So you've never even thought about kissing

Jordan?" Gaby asked.

"I haven't ever thought about kissing *anyone*. Jordan hasn't ever thought about kissing anyone, either. It's grosser than drinking fish poop," Priya insisted

"Yuck," Abby cried.

"Yeah, yuck," Candace echoed. She was kind of a human echo.

"What's yuck? The kissing or the fish poop?" Alex said.

"Both," Abby answered.

"With kissing a little higher on the yuck scale," Priya agreed.

"I wouldn't mind deciding for myself. With the right person," Brynn admitted.

"I still say Priya's found her perfect guy," Gaby said. "She's with Jordan practically every second possible. They spend all their free time together. And they've been in a ton of the same activities this summer. Like tomorrow, they both have nature together."

"We both like nature. So what?" Priya asked.

"All the magazines say it's good for couples to have things in common," Valerie joked, winking at Priya.

"Yeah, I bet if you and Jordan took that quiz from *Seventeen*, you'd definitely get ranked Much More Than Friends," Grace agreed.

"Just because we both like nature?" Priya protested. "Lots of people like nature! Grace is in nature with me, too." Luckily, they'd reached the bunk by then. "I call first shower!" Priya shouted, ending the conversation.

▲ ▲ ▲

"Bat!" Priya called out the next day during nature. The bandanna tied around her eyes made her blind as a . . . you know.

"Tree!" someone to her left answered.

"Moth!" someone behind her squeaked. She was positive it was Jordan, trying to disguise his voice.

Two other people called out "moth" from somewhere in front of her. She was pretty sure Grace was one of them, because of the Grace-like, but not moth-like, giggling.

Priya spun around in the direction the squeaky definitely-Jordan voice had come from. "Bat!" she called out again. She got answers of "tree" and "moth" from all around her, along with some more probably-Grace giggles. She focused on one particular "moth." This time it had been called out in a deep, booming voice. But Priya's best friend couldn't fool her. She knew him inside out. She'd been there at the most embarrassing moment of his life, and he'd been right there at hers. Jordan's—calling his second grade teacher "Mommy" in front of everybody. Priya's—peeing in her pants at Holly Perry's seventh birthday party after proving that she could chug a half gallon of lemonade without taking a breath (thanks very much for *that* dare, Jordan) and then getting really, really involved in a game of hide-and-seek.

"Bat! Bat! Bat!" Priya yelled. Arms outstretched, she stumbled toward the voice calling "moth" that she was sure was Jordan's. *Gotcha*, she thought. Then she launched herself into the darkness, and tackled . . . somebody . . . onto the grass. She jerked off her blindfold. Green eyes. Messy, longish brown hair. Freckles. Yep, it was Jordan.

"Great echolocation, Priya," Roseanne, the counselor in charge of the nature hut, called. "You guys see how the bat located its dinner? When Priya called 'bat,' that was like a bat sending out a sonar pulse. And when you guys answered, that was like the bat receiving the echoes from the pulse. That's how bats pinpoint where things are."

"I rule!" Priya shoved her fists into the air.

Jordan climbed to his feet. "Congratulations, bat girl. You just ate a moth."

"So? Good source of protein," Priya told him as she stood up.

"Priya's right," Roseanne agreed. She ran her fingers through her long curly hair, making it even more wild. Priya was glad her dark hair was short, short, short. Pretty much nothing she did could mess it up. "Insects are high in protein and low in fat and cholesterol. They are really nutritional. In fact, I have some chocolate-covered grasshoppers back in the nature shack if any of you want to try them," Roseanne continued.

"No thank you. I'm on a special diet. Nothing that hops," Grace joked. "I'm really missing the frog legs and kangaroo meat. But I've lost like an eighth of a quarter of a pound already." *Maybe if they were gummy grasshoppers she'd go for it*, Priya thought. Grace had a serious gummy bear habit.

"That is completely disgusting. And chocolate

does have fat," Chelsea, one of the Bunk 4A girls, decreed. She narrowed her eyes at Grace. "You might want to consider cutting out chocolate if you're serious about losing weight."

"But I'm not," Grace answered.

Priya shot Jordan a wicked smile. "I'm thinking three points," she whispered to him. No way would he let a grasshopper into his mouth, even one that was covered in sweet, chocolaty goodness. He was the Picky Eater poster boy. Jordan didn't even like the foods he *was* willing to eat to touch each other. He even brought a supply of those plastic picnic plates with three separate sections with him to camp so he could keep his food compartmentalized. Not just to camp, either.

"Eating the 'hopper would put you one point ahead of me," she added, just to torture him. As if he didn't totally know that already.

"How is that extreme?" Jordan asked. "How is that worthy of our challenge?"

"Oh, right." Priya shook her head. "You eat bugs every day. It's not extreme at all."

"You know what would be extreme?" Jordan asked, leaning close to her, his breath hot against her ear. "If you made me kiss someone."

Priya jerked back and stared at her best friend.

*Wh-what?* She felt herself blushing. Even though *she* wasn't the one who'd started babbling about kissing. Kissing. She didn't think she'd ever heard Jordan use the word before. Maybe she'd just had an ear malfunction. "Huh? I didn't hear you."

"You missed a moth," Jordan said. He whipped

out one foot, and she was face down in the grass before she had time to react.

"You see it?" he asked.

"No, do you?" Priya yanked him down next to her.

"Jordan. Priya. Playtime's over," Roseanne teased, but with an I-mean-it edge to her voice.

Now that was something Priya *and* Jordan had heard a bunch of times. They'd been hearing it their whole lives.

Priya scrambled up, managing to step on Jordan's foot accidentally-on-purpose. He grinned at her. And her world was normal again.

Except she knew she really hadn't had an ear malfunction. Jordan had used the K word. And just yesterday she'd told everyone in her bunk that Jordan had no interest in kissing anyone, ever.

Didn't she know her BBFF at all?

"Bug juice. I will perish of dehydration if Priya doesn't pass me the bug juice!" Brynn exclaimed.

"Priya!" Sarah, Alex, and Abby called together with their hands cupped around their mouths.

Priya blinked. "Huh?" She realized that she was holding a forkful of spaghetti halfway to her mouth. She also realized everyone at her table in the mess hall—which meant every girl in her bunk—was staring at her. "What?" she asked.

Sarah smiled. "Brynn has asked you for the bug juice, like, three times."

"Oh. Sorry." Priya passed the plastic pitcher of bright red bug juice across the table to Brynn.

"I'm going to live!" Brynn cried dramatically, green eyes all twinkly. Brynn pretty much said everything dramatically. She was really into theater. She'd just played Little Orphan Annie in a small camp production. She already had the red hair, but that's not why she got the part. And Priya was sure Brynn would get a part in the big camp production at the end of the summer. Brynn was really talented. Although sometimes it got annoying when she didn't keep the drama on the stage.

"What were you thinking about, anyway?" Alex asked Priya. "You were totally zonked."

Priya felt her cheeks get hot. She knew her face had to be turning red, even with her tan.

"She's blushing. It has to be good," Gaby observed. "We must make her tell." She smiled, looking over at Priya like she was hoping Priya would blush even more.

Priya took a mega bite of the spaghetti to give herself time to think. Should she tell them what had really been going through her brain? The girls in her bunk were pretty cool. But she didn't know them that well. Because, like they said, she spent almost all her free time with Jordan.

But what she'd been thinking about tonight . . . it was nothing she could talk to Jordan about. Because it was *about* Jordan.

"Well?" Gaby prompted as soon as Priya swallowed. The girl could be a little pushy. Geez.

"If she doesn't want to tell, she doesn't want to tell," Alex said, knocking a soccer ball back and forth between her feet under the table.

"No, it's okay," Priya told her, deciding to go for it. This sitch was probably something she could use the girl-POV on. Even back at home, she didn't hang with girls that much. She, Jordan, and her little brother—only one year littler—mostly did things together.

"Well?" Gaby said again, her lower lip sticking out in a pout. She always pouted when she didn't get what she wanted right when she wanted it. That or threw a tantrum.

Priya sucked in a deep breath. But she still didn't feel ready. So she took a long drink of bug juice. Choked on it. Then started to talk. "Um, you know that competition I have with Jordan?"

"As in the competition that has required three visits to Nurse Helen?" Becky, their counselor, asked. It wasn't all that much of a question.

"Uh-huh." Priya nodded. "But we aren't doing anything that might require a nurse anymore. I swear. So, anyway, I was telling him that I'd give him three points if he'd eat a grasshopper—"

"What?" Valerie burst out. Gaby's pout opened up into an O of surprise.

"Roseanne said she had chocolate-covered grasshoppers in the nature hut," Grace explained. "Priya wasn't going to just catch one in the field and make Jordan eat it with its legs kicking or anything."

"Oh, ew." Abby wrinkled her nose.

"Ew," Candace echoed.

"I'm sure they were sterilized or something," Grace reassured Becky. "Roseanne wouldn't offer us food—or whatever you call it—that would send us to the nurse."

"This doesn't have anything to do with the grass-hopper," Priya said quickly. "See, Jordan said something after I gave him the grasshopper challenge. Something, um, weird. I don't know what it means." Her words came out faster and faster. "Maybeitdoesn'tmeananything."

"You should sign up for drama next time," Brynn said loudly and slowly. "You need to do some work on your e-nun-ci-a-tion." She winked.

"So tell us what he said already," Gaby ordered.

Priya reached for her glass of bug juice again, then told herself not to be such a chicken. "He said that if I wanted to give him a really extreme challenge, I should make him kiss someone."

Sophie, their CIT, put a bowl of sort of old looking fruit on their table and lingered, ears wide open.

"Ooooh." Grace leaned closer.

"Yeah, ooooh," Candace said.

"I need more details," Valerie told Priya. "Was there anyone else in the group when you two were talking about the kissing thing?"

"No," Priya answered. "He didn't exactly whisper it. But he leaned in. He was definitely only talking to me. I thought maybe my ears were full of wax. Or, actually, I was hoping that was it. I was hoping I didn't hear him right. But I know I did. I know that he said I should make him *kiss* someone. And Jordan's never,

ever used that word before. Maybe he doesn't know what it means. You think that could be it? I heard him right, but he meant something totally else? Like, I don't know, he wants to play a variation of dodgeball with somebody."

"*Kiss* is a one syllable word," Valerie said. "I think you learn it when you're, like, two."

"Uh-huh. It's like I said," Gaby burst out. "Maybe Jordan isn't your boyfriend right now. But he wants to be! I was right!"

"It does sound as if Jordan *liiiikes* you," Sarah said. And Sarah should know. She'd just found out that this guy David liked her.

"Sounds like maybe he even wants to kiss you," Abby added. "As gross as that is."

"Priya and Jordan, climbing a tree," Brynn began with a grin.

"K-I-S-S-I-N-G," Grace and Valerie joined in, giggling.

"No way. We're buds, compadres, amigos, uh, pals, um . . ." Priya's voice trailed off. She couldn't think of any more words.

"Mates, chums," Grace volunteered as she peeled one of the mushy bananas.

"Jordan's my best friend," Priya told the group, going for the simple truth. "You don't go around kissing your best friend." Because if you did, they wouldn't be your best friend anymore. And she couldn't imagine her world without Jordan as her best friend. Even trying to think about it made her feel empty inside.

"But wasn't there that movie with Ashton Kutcher

and Amanda somebody where they're best friends and then they fall in love?" Sophie asked.

"Yeah," Valerie answered. "So just because he's your friend, doesn't mean he couldn't end up feeling something else," she told Priya.

"You guys, you're freakin' me out. And I was already freaked out because I thought that what Jordan said meant he was ready to jump into the boyfriend/girlfriend thing with some girl. I was weirded out thinking he wanted to kiss *any* girl. Forget about me!"

"Maybe he *was* just talking about kissing in a general kind of way," Alex said. "Don't go into a total meltdown."

"Right. You're right. I'll try to stay solid." Priya sucked in a deep breath. "Here's another theory. Jordan and I are always daring each other to do extreme things. Right before he brought up the kissing thing, I'd just dared him to eat a grasshopper. So maybe he was just trying to think of something worse and kissing was the worst thing he could come up with."

*Yeah. That makes total sense,* Priya thought. *Except for that part where Jordan goes into a minor freak if his mashed potatoes touch his salad dressing. Eating a grasshopper has to be very, very high on his list of worsts.*

"And that was the very worst thing he could come up with?" Valerie shook her head, her braids flopping around her face. "That would make him one sick boy. I mean, there are many bad things in the world."

"Would it really be so absolutely, completely terrible to be boyfriend/girlfriend with Jordan? I mean, it's been pretty clear all summer he's into you," Sarah said, and Priya was horrified to see half her table nodding in agreement. Her bunkmates always teased her about Jordan. But she thought they were just . . . just teasing. She never thought any of them really believed there was something going on between them.

"Maybe not the kissing thing. At least not right away," Sarah added. A slight blush crept up her neck and into her cheeks. "I definitely wanted to punch David when I first thought he liked me, but now it's really cool."

"But you guys weren't ever best friends like me and Jordan," Priya answered. "You found out pretty fast that he liked you liked you. And he probably knew from the beginning. Jordan—he's almost like my brother. I know you guys always laugh when I say that. But I've seen him pick his nose, okay?"

"Too much information," Abby cried.

"Yeah, too much," Candace agreed.

"Yeah, I think I'll take myself back to the kitchen now," Sophie said. She gave them a little wave as she hurried away.

"I just couldn't think of him as a boyfriend," Priya said. She let out a long sigh. "Anyway, he was probably just kidding around. Right?"

Nobody answered fast enough for her.

"Right," Priya said, answering her own question. But not quite convincing herself.

Priya headed out of the mess hall and turned toward the rec room, then hesitated. After dinner there was always some free time before whatever activity was on for the night, and she and Jordan and a few guys from his bunk usually met up for a game of Spoons, this card game where the winner could make the loser eat a spoonful of whatever they wanted (as long as it was food). It was very hard on the loser if the loser was a wimpy food freakazoid named Jordan. Not that he lost that often. He was excellent at Spoons. Priya was pretty darn good herself. Most the time they both ended up stealthing it over to the kitchen to whip up something disgusting for some loser to choke down.

It was always total fun. Except . . . except tonight, especially after her discussion with the girls of 4C, there would be a big ick factor to hanging with Jordan. What if he brought up kissing again? Or just looked at her in a *like her* like her way? Or looked at any girl in the rec center in a like like way? She might puke—before she even had to eat one spoonful of whatever.

Sarah, Valerie, and Grace headed by. "Hey!" Priya said, way too loudly. "Um, what are you guys doing tonight?"

"We're going to make some lanyards," Sarah answered, sounding a little surprised. Maybe because Priya had never shown any interest in their free-time plans before. She hung with her bunkmates during the bunk activities—and had a lot of fun with them. But her free time was Jordan, Jordan, and more Jordan. "We want to see if you can make them out of licorice whips—you know, those really thin ones. Grace got some in a care package."

"You want to make some, too?" Grace asked.

"I don't know how," Priya admitted. Lanyard-making was way too tame for the Who's-the-Most-Extreme Challenge, even though practically everyone at camp made them, and traded them, and gave them to their friends.

"It's totally easy," Valerie told her. "We can teach you."

They seemed like they really wanted her to say yes. Hanging with the girls—it could be okay. And even if the lanyard thing was sort of boring, there wouldn't be any ick factor.

Why did Jordan have to go and mess everything up? Why couldn't things be the way they had before? When she knew exactly what it would be like to hang with him? When there was zero possibility of an ick factor? When she could still trust her very best friend to act like her very best friend?

But she couldn't. She couldn't totally trust Jordan anymore.

"That would be great!" Priya exclaimed. "Let's do it!"

chapter

# TWO

Priya pulled in a deep lungful of morning air, waiting for Dr. Steve to get the Wednesday flag-raising started. It was like she was absorbing part of the sunrise into her body. How could anybody not be a morning person? She started to suck in another breath—then her chest tightened, and tightened, and *tightened*. Until there was no room for any O2. Not even a molecule.

The sight of Jordan approaching the flagpole made it impossible for her to breathe. She hadn't seen him since yesterday at dinner. Hadn't talked to him since he used the K word. Last night, she'd told Becky she had a stomach-ache and bailed on the singdown scheduled after free time. She just hadn't been able to deal with the possibility of another up close and personal encounter with Jordan yesterday.

*Which Jordan is that over there by the flagpole?* Priya wondered. *Normal Jordan? Or the Jordan who wants to talk about kissing all the time? Okay, once. But still. Is it normal Jordan? Or weird Jordan?* Her best friend? Or somebody else?

"You all right?" Alex whispered. Alex always seemed to notice how everybody was feeling.

Priya nodded, and the motion seemed to let some air into her lungs. She forced herself to keep her eyes on Jordan. He looked . . . normal. Yeah. Half asleep, like always. Jordan didn't fully come alive until after breakfast. Also, like always, he was wearing one of the t-shirts he'd swiped from his older brother's collection minutes before they left for camp. This one said "My Dog Can Lick Anyone." Priya smiled. That was stupid. And funny. Just like Jordan. More air entered her lungs, and her chest uncrunched.

He was probably just being stupid and funny with that kissing comment yesterday. He'd probably be totally normal when they had nature together this afternoon.

Probably.

"Okay, I need you to partner up," Roseanne called when the group was gathered in the nature shack that afternoon.

Jordan knocked shoulders with Priya, assuming they'd team it. He was still exhibiting signs of normalcy. As usual, he was chomping on a wad of banana gum that could choke a whale. And, also as usual, his sneakers were emitting an odor that was noxious enough to kill off a raccoon. Not that Priya cared. Her own sneakers didn't smell so great, but she did spray them down with Lysol once in a while.

"I know that you've probably all done scavenger

hunts at camp," Roseanne said, "but today we're going to do one that's a little different." She walked around the room, handing a list to each team. "Everything you'll be looking for can be found in nature."

"We are going to rock this," Jordan told Priya.

"Totally," she agreed. He was acting normal, so she was starting to feel pretty normal, too. And relieved. Big-time relieved.

"The team that gets back here with all the items first wins a prize," Roseanne added.

"If it's a box of chocolate-covered grasshoppers, I'll be moving very, very slowly," Grace called out with a grin.

"Would I do that to you?" Roseanne teased. She shook her head. "No grasshoppers. Or ants. Or other insects. I promise. Oh, and I forgot to say, it's okay to bring things back to show for the scavenger hunt, obviously. There are specimen buckets against the wall. But treat the great outdoors gently, all right? You know the motto—"

"Be nice to nature," the group said along with Roseanne.

"Right. Now, on your marks, get set—go!" Roseanne cried.

Priya and Jordan bolted for the specimen buckets. They each grabbed one and were the first team out the door. "Let's do the search on the trail that loops around the lake," Priya suggested.

"You got it, chief," Jordan answered as they ran.

Chief. She could deal with that. Chief, captain, supreme ruler of the universe—all good. So were buddy, pal, compadre, amigo, mate, and whatever that other one Grace had come up with was. Just not girlfriend.

Jordan skidded to a halt when they hit the lakeside trail. "We gotta slow down or we'll miss stuff."

"Yep," Priya agreed. "So read me the list."

"Smooth rock, smooth-edged leaf, something that feels nice, Y-shaped stick, someone's food, a pebble smaller than a pea, something prickly, something with four legs, something that you could use as a natural spoon," Jordan rattled off.

"I have half a piece of toast in my pocket, but I guess that's not the kind of 'someone's food' Roseanne was thinking of," Priya told him. Toast was the Lakeview chef's specialty. Priya always tried to grab at least an extra piece to get her through the grossness of the rest of the food.

"Jordan want toast. Give toast Jordan," he said, doing his Frankenstein imitation.

Priya pulled the toast out of her pocket and jammed the whole thing in her mouth. "Oh, I'm sorry. Was this what you wanted?" she asked sweetly, giving him a good look at the mushy bread.

"You are damaged," Jordan told her. "And where were you last night? I had a completely repulsive mixture all planned out for your first defeat. Did you get tired of losing or what?"

"The girls in my bunk, uh, wanted to do this thing together," Priya said. It was the first time she'd lied to Jordan. It made her feel like she'd just eaten a gallon of whatever disgusting mixture he'd had planned for her. What was the point of having a best friend if you lied to him?

"I thought I saw Sarah and David," Jordan commented.

"Yeah, I had to be there early to . . . help with set up for the . . . thing," Priya answered quickly, hoping she didn't sound as phony to Jordan as she did to herself.

"You weren't at the singdown, either," Jordan said. "I would have heard your beautiful voice from anywhere." Jordan always teased her about her voice. It was anti-beautiful.

"After the thing, I got a stomachache, so I got permission to go to bed early." Geez, now a lie on top of a lie. She wanted to confess everything. Everything except for the reason for the lies. She didn't want to go there with Jordan. She wanted to erase that moment from history. Just snip out that one moment when Jordan brought up kissing.

"Hey, I see one of the things on the list!" Jordan carefully stepped off the path. "Close you eyes," he told Priya.

"O-kay," she said, shutting her eyes. *Wait, is he going to kiss me?* came the sudden, unwelcome thought. Was this what a first kiss was like? She'd never thought about it. She'd never talked about it with girlfriends. She didn't really have girlfriends like that. Did a boy just tell you to shut your eyes—and do it?

*No,* Priya told herself. *That's not what's happening. He's being all normal. You're crazy. And when he was talking about the kissing, he wasn't necessarily talking about kissing you. Or anybody. He was just kidding around.*

But every muscle in her face tensed. Her lips tightened into a skinny line. Then she felt it . . . something soft, and smooth, and wet, and cool against her cheek. "Feels good, doesn't it?" Jordan asked.

The cool wet thing was still pressed against her skin—so it couldn't be his mouth, 'cause he'd be using his mouth for talking. She relaxed a tiny bit. "Yeah, sorta," she admitted.

"Open 'em up," Jordan ordered.

Her eyes snapped open. And she saw the snail Jordan was holding up against her face, its soft, smooth, wet, cool snail body against her skin. Priya let out a snort of laughter. "That's one down. Let's find the rest," she told him. Her bones all felt as soft as the snail. That's how relieved she was.

If Jordan had kissed her, that would have been it. Friendship over. She'd never be able to look at him again. Forget about talk to him. It would have been too . . . humiliating. And weird. And just wrong.

Jordan put the snail into his specimen bucket. Priya added a pine needle to hers. "Smooth-edged leaf," she noted. "A pine needle counts as a leaf, right?"

"I'm pretty sure," Jordan said.

"We should divide up the area." Priya swung her bucket back and forth as she walked. "You take the ground to the left of the trail. I'll take the right."

"Cool." Jordan started to scan the ground to the left of the trail. "You know that guy Zach from my bunk?"

"Yeah." Priya paused. She thought she'd seen a Y-shaped branch. She crouched down. Nope. It was a short branch lying at an angle against this longer one. She stood up. "What about him?"

"He never heard that you can light your farts. Can you believe that? I mean, every other guy in the bunk knew. You know, right?"

"I've known since kindergarten," Priya answered. "Where's Zach from? Where in the United States can you grow up without knowing that fart gas is flammable?" This was the great part about having a BBFF. Girls just didn't have conversations like this.

"Someplace in Florida. There's no excuse for it," Jordan said. "Hey, an acorn, that counts as someone's food." He grabbed it and tossed it into his bucket.

"So this guy Zach, how are his burping skills?" Priya asked. "I'm not talking advanced, like burping the alphabet. But can he at least do his name? I mean, it's only one syllable."

"No data on that," Jordan answered.

"Well, you gotta get some, pronto. If he has no skills, then I'm thinking an alien has taken over his body," Priya teased. She knew the conversation was totally moronic. But that was the best kind.

"An evil alien planning some kind of invasion?" Jordan asked.

"That's what I'm thinking." Priya checked out another possible Y-shaped stick. No go.

"One point if you burp the pledge of allegiance at lunch," Jordan challenged.

Priya reluctantly shook her head. "You can't do that kind of burping on bug juice, my friend."

*My* best *friend.*

"It's Barbeque Night, Barbeque Night," Brynn sang to the tune of "Halloween Town" from *The Nightmare Before Christmas*. "No need to take fright. It's Barbeque Night." She leaped and twirled down the aisle between the beds.

Priya knew exactly why Brynn and everybody else was so excited over the BBQ. She didn't know if the outdoor grills were easier for Pete, the cook, to use or what—but the hot dogs and hamburgers he served up at BBQs were much tastier than his indoor cooking. Tasty enough to be almost edible.

"There might be a need to take fright," Alex said. "It's a full moon. And one of the counselors always tells a creepy story at the campfire when there's a full moon." Alex had been a Lakeview camper forever. She knew the scoopage on everything. Although Priya and the campers who were back for a second or third summer knew a few things, too. Like the full moon deal.

Brynn flopped down on Sarah's bed. "Cool. I love scary stories. Have you heard the one about—"

The door to the bunk flew open. "I now interrupt the regularly scheduled programming for an important news bulletin," Valerie announced.

"Um, Val, *Brynn's* the drama queen," Grace joked. "I'm the funny one. Priya's the tomboy. Gaby's the—"

"The tomboy's going to want to hear this. And I bet the rest of you are, too," Valerie interrupted.

Gaby looked doubtful as she smoothed on a coat of strawberry pink lip gloss.

Valerie turned to Priya. "Remember what we were talking about last night at dinner? You know, what it meant when Jordan brought up kissing?"

"Didn't we already decide that it meant he liiiikes Priya?" Gaby asked, sounding bored.

"Oh, no we didn't," Priya answered. "And anyway, Jordan was totally normal today. Regular old Jordan. I'm now completely positive he was just kidding around," she told the group. "He has no interest in any girl—including me—except as a friend."

"Don't bet on it," Valerie said, brown eyes shining. "At least don't bet anything you're not hoping to get rid of. I ran into Natalie on my way over, and she said Simon said that Jordan was asking the guys in his bunk for advice. On girls. Make that girlfriends and how to get them."

"Wow," Abby said.

"That's . . . wow," Candace said.

"But, like I said, Jordan was acting completely the way he always does," Priya said. "He didn't mention the K word or anything like that." Her voice got higher with every word. She hoped no one noticed. "He talked about farts, okay? That's the level of normal I'm talking."

"Again with the too much information." Abby shook her head.

"Too much," Candace agreed.

"The only reason he went into bodily function territory was 'cause he hadn't gotten the lowdown from his crew," Grace offered. "The boy didn't know any better."

Sophie stuck her head into the bunk. "Let's move it out, girls. You know how fast the chow moves at barbeques."

Priya stood up and followed the other girls outside. The sky was going all pinky-purpley-orangey as the sun set, and she could already smell the smoke from the barbeque. But her stomach felt as if it was filled with grasshoppers. Live ones, not the chocolate-covered kind.

*Just chill. Maybe the whole thing got garbled when it got passed from Simon to Natalie to Valerie to everyone in 4C,* Priya told herself. *Remember when you went to Shelly Barone's stupid birthday party in the third grade and you played that stupid game telephone—instead of something fun like kickball or freeze tag? The whole point was that the message got all messed up as it went from person to person.*

*Yeah, that's probably the deal,* Priya thought as she got in the hamburger line. Then Gaby elbowed her in the side and nodded toward the closest hot dog line. And the grasshoppers in Priya's stomach started doing some extreme hip-hop moves.

Jordan had changed his t-shirt. Which was bizzaro enough. If Jordan had some kind of mega-spill or whatever, he'd *maybe* turn his tee inside out before dinner. Maybe. If he thought about it.

But the really bizzaro part was what he'd changed into. A whatchamacallit—polo shirt. With a collar and everything. Priya hadn't known that Jordan even owned one. Was he wearing it to impress a girl? Was he wearing it for *her?* Because he was going to attempt to become her *boyfriend?*

"The guys in his bunk don't exactly read *Vogue*," Gaby commented. "The outfit's passable. But what did they have him put in his hair—corn syrup?"

Priya raised her eyes up from the polo shirt. Jordan's brown hair was slicked down—and weirdly shiny. She had no idea how he'd gotten it that way. The most she attempted with her own hair was—well, nothing. That's why she liked it short. You couldn't really do anything with it but brush it.

"Oooh. Look at loverboy," Grace teased from her spot in front of Priya. "He's gonna make his move tonight. Maybe not on you. But on someone."

"No way," Priya said. But what else was she supposed to think? Grace had to be right. This had to be girl-related. What other reason could Jordan have for creating this . . . spectacle? It couldn't be that he thought he'd be given more burgers at the BBQ.

On autopilot, she grabbed a paper plate and held it out for a burger and some corn on the cob. She loved corn on the cob. But the melting butter on top reminded her of the gunk on Jordan's hair, and that got the grasshoppers all excited again, and she realized there was no way she was going to be able to force any food in there with them.

Priya sat down on one end of a fallen log, next to Brynn. A whole bunch of logs were arranged in circles around the big pit they used for camp-wide campfires. She stared at her full plate. "Anybody want seconds?" she asked, holding up her plate of firsts.

"Maybe. But I've only taken about two bites of what I've got," Alex answered from the next log over.

"Aren't you feeling good?" Becky asked from her spot next to Alex. Her blue eyes were wide with concern.

"I'm good. Just not that hungry," Priya said quickly.

"Everyone loses their appetite when they're in like," Grace joked from the other side of Brynn. Usually Priya thought Grace was funny. Usually.

"Everyone loses their appetite," Candace agreed, straddling the log in front of Priya's.

"I'm totally not in like," Priya snapped.

"Well somebody is," Brynn commented. "Somebody keeps staring over here. Somebody named Jordan."

And it was true. Jordan was gawking at her from one of the fallen logs on the opposite side of the huge campfire. The shadows thrown on his face by the flames made him look like a stranger. That and the freaky hair. And the *polo* shirt. The thing didn't even have a slogan on it. Priya jerked her eyes off him.

Why her? It would be bad if Jordan had started crushing on any girl. Because . . . because then everything would change. And Priya liked things exactly how they were, exactly the way they'd always been.

But out of all the girls around, why did Jordan have to liiike her? It just made it so much more gross. It would be gross to see Jordan looking at any girl with goo-goo eyes. But to feel him looking at her that way, that was gross squared. She took a quick peek at him. Yeah, he was definitely staring in her direction. Yikes.

"Maybe just try a few bites," Becky suggested in

concerned-counselor mode. "I don't want the sound of your stomach growling to wake everybody up in the middle of the night."

Priya figured it was easier to eat a little than argue. She picked up her corn on the cob and scraped some of the sweet corn off with her teeth. Grasshoppers would probably rather eat corn than hamburger, right?

She shot another glance at Jordan. She didn't want to, but she couldn't stop herself. He definitely wasn't having any trouble eating. He was heading over to the barbeque pits for another hot dog. Whatever. At least he wasn't still mooning at her with big moo-cow eyes. She managed another bite of corn.

"Incoming!" Alex called from her place next to Candace.

Priya automatically jerked up her head, looking for the baseball or football or Frisbee that should be flying toward her.

"Not that kind," Alex said. "Boy incoming."

Incoming like a bomb. There he was. Jordan. Candace and Alex scooted closer together so he could sit down on their log across from Brynn and Priya. "Hey," Priya muttered, goosebumps appearing on her arms, even though it wasn't that cold. She felt as if every single girl in her bunk was staring at her, like she had suddenly sprouted a second head or something.

"How is everyone enjoying their food?" Jordan asked, staring down at his deck shoes.

First—"How is everyone enjoying their food?" What was he, some kind of lobotomized cruise director? Second—deck shoes. True, his sneaks reeked. But

Jordan was kinda proud of the stench they'd accumulated. Those shoes weren't his, Priya was sure of it. She felt her two bites of corn try to come back up her throat.

"Yummy in the tummy," Brynn said, since Priya hadn't answered.

Jordan laughed. Hard. As hard as that time at swimming when Priya had floated on her back and pretended her belly button was a whale's blowhole.

Brynn started to giggle. "Yummy in the tummy," Jordan repeated, and he actually giggled himself. Yes, giggled. Then he straightened the collar of his polo shirt and glanced at Priya.

She had to help him. Jordan was in there somewhere. Trapped under the clothes and the hair and the cruise-director speak and the giggling. She just needed to bust him loose.

Light bulb. Priya leaned across Grace. "Hey, Gaby," she whispered. "Do you have one of your secret stash of Cokes with you?"

Gaby checked out Becky and Sophie to make sure they weren't listening—although they didn't mind the girls having some junk food contraband inside the bunk, as long as the campers were willing to share with them. "Yes. But it's for me, as in M-E."

"What if I do whatever comes up for you on the chore wheel tomorrow?" Priya asked. "Then who's it for?"

Gaby slapped a lukewarm can of Coke into Priya's hand. Priya slipped it to Jordan. "Give a point if you burp the camp motto here and now," she challenged.

"That's gross," Brynn said.

Jordan tossed the can back to Priya. "I'll pass."

Dylan, the counselor for 4F, stood up. "Quiet down, everyone. Quiet. I'm about to tell you a story—a true story. It's what happened to a bride, a bride who always wore a black velvet collar," he called. "And I have to warn you that her story is intense. So I need you to keep an eye on your neighbors. Campers have been known to faint when they hear the story. If you see someone near you getting pale or having trouble breathing, shoot up your hand, and one of the counselors will be right over to help. The story is that frightening."

*More frightening than the fact that Jordan has clearly been taken over by an alien?* Priya thought.

chapter

THREE

"They're both asleep," Sarah whispered late that night after she did a Sophie-and-Becky bed check.

Priya climbed out of the top bunk as quietly as possible and joined the circle of girls gathering in the middle of the cabin. "Everybody knows how to play, right?" Gaby asked as they sat down.

"I don't," Priya answered.

"Me either," Abby said.

Gaby rolled her eyes. *Geez*, Priya thought. Could Priya help it if she hung with boys, and boys didn't play this "I Never" game, whatever it was?

"Okay, Alex is handing out the candy that we use as tokens," Gaby went on.

"The Lifesavers are sugar-free, if anyone cares," Alex said, as she gave eleven of the individually wrapped candies to each girl. Alex only ate treats without sugar because she had juvenile diabetes.

"How it works is, we go around the circle. Each person says something they've never done—but it should be something they think a lot of the rest of us *have* done," Gaby explained. "If you've done what the person says they haven't, you have to put one of your candies in the middle of the circle. Once all your candy is gone, you're out of the game. The winner is the one who still has candy left at the end. We go around the circle as many times as it takes to eliminate all but one of us."

Priya nodded. She got it. It didn't exactly sound exciting. Or even fun. But she got it. And maybe it would keep her mind off Jordan and his BBQ freak show. It's not like she'd have been able to sleep after that. And everyone else was a little tense after the story Dylan told about the bride and her black velvet choker and the way her head plopped right down onto the staircase when she finally took the choker off, which she was never, never, ever supposed to do.

"I'll go first," Gaby said. She tilted her head to one side, thinking. "I never had a birthday party at my house."

"Come on!" Sarah protested.

"Shhh!" Grace pointed toward the part of the bunk where Becky and Sophie slept.

"It's true," Gaby insisted. "Even my first birthday party wasn't one of those home ones with crepe paper streamers. It was at a tea shoppe. That's with an 'e' at the end."

"Oooh. Fancy. And I mean that with an 'e' at the end," Grace said.

Sarah tossed a piece of candy into the center of the circle. So did every other girl. "I never go anywhere that doesn't have an 'e' at the end would probably have worked just as well," she commented.

Gaby gave a cat-who-just-scarfed-a-gallon-of-cream smile. Then she turned to Alex, who sat on her right. "Go," she instructed.

Alex nibbled her lower lip. "I never . . . I never got my period."

About a third of the girls tossed in candy. Priya wasn't one of them.

She was a little surprised. She thought practically every girl in her school had started. It was good to spend some time in an X-chromosome-only situation. You could learn a few things. Priya grinned trying to imagine discussing her period with her little brother. Or Jordan.

She shoved the thought of Jordan out of her head. This game was about distraction from the horror.

"That wasn't as good a one as mine," Gaby told Alex. Gaby had been one of the candy-tossers. "You should have known at least some of us would have gotten our period. You have to choose more unique stuff if you want to win."

Alex gave a little shrug. "I just wanted to know," she admitted. "I was hoping I wasn't the last one to, you know . . . get it."

Priya had just learned something else from the girly game. She wasn't the only girl who worried about not having gotten her period. Not that she wanted it.

Not exactly. But she wanted it if everyone else had already gotten it.

"I'm glad you used the period thing for your turn," Abby said. "I wanted to know, too. I haven't gotten mine either, and I keep obsessing. I don't know if I should ask my mom to take me to a doctor or what. But I don't want a doctor to do whatever they'd have to do to test me."

"Lots of people our age don't have it yet," Sarah told her. "Look at the candy pile. Not even half of us put in candy for that one. So a lot of us are in the 'I never' group."

Abby nodded. "Yeah. I guess I just got worried because my best friend at school got hers when she was ten."

"Ten!" Priya burst out at the same time as Valerie.

"Yeah," Abby insisted.

"I don't know what's going on with mine," Sarah admitted. "I got it once, then I kinda got it one other time. Then nothing."

"In health, they said that's normal at the beginning," Priya said. It felt good to have something to offer to the conversation.

"It should have an official start day. So you could be completely prepared," Valerie said, getting nods from everyone.

"My turn," Grace said after a moment. She glanced around the circle, like she was trying to read each girl's mind. When she spoke, her voice was low, and deep, and intense. "I never . . . never . . . ever . . .

took off my black velvet choker."

"Not funny!" Abby whisper-screamed. "I can totally see that bride's head bouncing down the stairs."

Priya bit down on the inside of her cheek to stop herself from launching into a loud hee-haw fit. Abby's eyes were so wide they looked almost ready to fall out of their sockets.

"I don't think any of us should have to give up candy for that one," Gaby said, sounding annoyed because Grace wasn't taking the game—*her* game—seriously.

"That wasn't my real turn," Grace protested.

"Yes, it was," Gaby insisted.

"Who votes that Grace gets another go—this time only?" Alex asked. Everyone but Gaby and Abby raised their hands.

"Okay, seriously, I never went to pre-school," Grace told the group.

"Good one." Priya applauded softly as everyone was forced to toss in a Lifesaver.

"My mom has this whole kids-should-be-kids theory," Grace said.

"That explains a lot about you," Valerie teased. Grace tossed a Lifesaver at her. "I'm keepin' it," Val said, catching it in the air.

"No fair," Grace protested. "I didn't lose that because I did an 'I never.'"

Alex held up her hands. "I'm staying out of it this time."

"You can't use that Lifesaver in the game," Gaby told Valerie, reaching for the candy.

"Fine." Valerie quickly unwrapped the Lifesaver and popped it in her mouth. "Purple. My fave."

Priya snorted a laugh. She was starting to really like Val's style.

"My go," Sarah said. "I never had a boy ask me to go to the Potomac Cruise Dance with him."

Nobody threw in a Lifesaver.

"Do you understand how to play this game?" Gaby demanded, glaring at Sarah.

"Shhh!" Grace put her finger to her lips.

"But everybody is going on the cruise, right?" Abby asked, eyes wide. "I know we get to choose activities for the other days, so we'll be in different groups. But everyone's going on the cruise, so why would we need to be invited?"

"We don't," Alex told her.

"We don't," Sarah repeated. "It's just that some guys are asking girls. There's going to be swing dance lessons, so it'll be kind of like a camp dance. You can go without a date. Or you can go with one. I just wondered if anyone else was going with one."

Priya had almost forgotten about it the dancing part of the cruise. How was she going to deal with a dance without normal Jordan to make it fun? There had been some dances at their school last year, but she and Jordan hadn't gone. They'd hung with Sammy, watching horror movies or playing in these massive hide-and-seek games with Sammy and his friends.

Maybe she and Jordan hung out with Sammy so much because Sammy was sick a lot when he was little. He'd had to skip a lot of school, and had had a ton of doctors' appointments. Priya almost always had to come straight home after she got out of school because her mom had to cart her along to whatever appointment Sammy had. So no after-school stuff for Priya. No going over to other kids' houses. But when they got back from the doctor of the moment, there was always Jordan next door. For her and Sammy. Even when Sammy got totally better, the three of them kept on doing everything together.

"*Some* guys are asking. What guys other than David? Obviously David is going to ask you, right?" Gaby said.

Sarah shrugged. "I'm not sure. He said some other guys were asking people."

"But it's okay just to go alone, right?" Abby asked. "Girls can dance in groups, right?"

"Of course," Valerie said. "I don't think I'll be going with anyone."

"Oh, who cares," Gaby muttered. "Come on. Let's play. Abby, your turn. Make it good."

"Hmmm. I never had a boy crush on me. Forget about having a boy ask me to the Potomac Dance," Abby said.

A few girls tossed Lifesavers into the circle. Priya wasn't one of them.

Grace gave a muffled yelp. Gaby shook her head, her eyebrows raised. Brynn reached across the circle with her foot and gave Priya a light kick.

"We're not going to let you get away with that," Valerie informed Priya. "We all witnessed Jordan full-on crushing tonight. On *you*, missy."

There were nods and uh-huhs all around.

Priya scrubbed her face—her hot, red face—with her fingers. "Jordan did seem like he was trying to get *someone's* attention tonight, with the shoes and the hair and everything. I'll give you that. So I guess he wasn't just joking around with that kissing comment. I guess he really has lost his mind and decided he's in liiike. But you don't know it's with me." She pointed at Val. "You didn't witness that, and neither did anybody else."

"When loverboy was laughing too loud at nothing—which is *so* the behavior of a boy with a crush—he was sitting right across from you," Gaby said. "He picked that seat all by himself."

"And we all saw him staring at you before he finally came over," Grace added. "I'll sign an affidavit or whatever they're called."

"I think you have to face the truth, Priya," Alex told her. "Jordan wants to be your boyfriend, not your best friend."

Slowly, Priya pushed her Lifesaver into the circle.

▲ ▲ ▲

"Are you really sure you're feeling okay?" Becky asked Priya the next night at dinner.

"Uh-huh, yep," she answered, then struggled to choke down a second bite of Thursday's special—watery lasagna.

Jordan had shown up to the mess hall in another *outfit*—khakis, striped polo shirt, deck shoes. But that wasn't what was keeping her from eating this time. Or at least, not the main thing. What *was* keeping her from eating were her after-dinner plans.

There was a chance—maybe just a teeny-weeny chance, but a chance—that the girls in her bunk were wrong about Jordan crushing on her. And tonight, after dinner, during their regular card game, Priya was going to find out. Who would be able to eat right before that?

"He's looking at you again," Brynn whispered from her seat to Priya's left.

"I'll be a witness to that," Grace joked from Priya's right.

Great. She was surrounded.

"His hair's a little better tonight. That's something," Gaby commented from across the table.

Totally surrounded.

"Isn't there anything else to talk about?" Priya exclaimed.

"World peace?" Valerie suggested.

"Boring," Gaby said.

"Color war?" Sophie suggested as she dropped off a basket of bread.

"Too far away. And we don't even know if we'll be on the same team," Alex answered.

"Sorry, Priya, we'll have to keep talking about you and your boyfriend," Grace said.

"I thought I heard some mice in the bunk last night," Becky commented casually.

"Mice?" Abby exclaimed.

"Wait. Did you say mice?" Candace asked.

"Well, a kind of rustling sound. Sort of like candy

wrappers. I thought maybe it was mice. What do you think?" Becky asked.

*Thanks, Becky*, Priya thought. *I really needed that subject change.* She ate another bite of lasagna just because she thought she owed her counselor one.

"Mice, definitely mice," Grace said. "Mice with little black velvet chokers."

"Grace! Do you have to keep bringing that up?" Abby burst out. "I'm only a little less afraid of mice than I am of headless brides."

"But you know there weren't any mice in the bunk. You know we—" Alex stopped. "I mean, I know because I got up to go to the bathroom in the middle of the night and I would have seen them if there were any to see," she said quickly, shooting a glance at Becky.

"Well, that's a relief," Becky said. "I wouldn't want poor little mice heads plopping off all over our floor."

"Becky!" Abby wailed.

"Sorry, sorry," Becky told her. "But come on, you can't believe that story. No one's head could have been held on by a choker."

"I have an announcement to make," Brynn said, as if she were standing on a stage. She waited until everyone at the 4C table was looking at her. Her green eyes sparkled as she continued. "Jordan is still staring at Priya."

Grace held up her hand. "I'm a witness."

Priya was surrounded. She had the sudden urge to just put her head down—right in her plate of lasagna if necessary.

Priya snatched up the cards Jordan passed to her. She needed either a six of clubs and a six of hearts, or she needed a four of hearts. There was nothing in Jordan's pile she could use. She hurled them at Spence.

*Come on, come on, come on,* she thought, impatient. *Where are my cards, Jordan?* She shot a look at him, and realized he was holding a spoon. Priya slid one of the two spoons remaining in the middle of the table into her hand, while hurling a few cards in Spence's direction to keep him distracted.

Who would notice that the game was over first and grab the last spoon—Spence or Joe? They were both totally focused on their cards. Jordan shot her a few cards from his hand, Priya snatched them up, like she was dying for them, then slapped them down next to Spence. Joe gave a grunt of frustration as he sent three cards in Jordan's direction.

Jordan gave Priya a fast, secret, look-at-those-two-goofballs smile, and she smiled back. Because for one second, in the middle of the craziness of the game, she'd forgotten. She'd forgotten her best friend had had a brain, personality, and wardrobe transplant.

Priya caught a flash of movement out of the corner of her eye as Spence's hand snaked out and captured the last spoon. He kept passing cards to Joe, and Joe frantically sent cards to Jordan who sent them along to Spence, who sent them right back to Joe. Finally, Joe got it.

"How long?" Joe moaned. "How long this time?"

"At least a full minute since I got my beauty," Spence told him, caressing his plastic spoon.

"Who was first?" Joe demanded.

"One of those two." Spence nodded toward Priya and Jordan.

"Why did I even ask?" Joe let the cards in his hand flutter down onto the table.

"Even Priya was slow tonight," Jordan said. "I thought we were going to be playing this one hand until the rec center closed." He stood up. "Want to help with the concoction?" he asked Priya.

It would give her the chance to be alone with him. Which would give her the chance to find out what she needed to find out. "Sure," she answered, the word coming out in a squeak.

"Prepare to puke," Jordan warned Joe.

"I'm so scared," Joe called after Priya and Jordan as they hurried out of the rec center.

*No, I'm so scared*, Priya thought. She sucked in a deep breath, trying to get a grip. *Okay, so just spit it out*, Priya coached herself on the way to the mess hall. *'Jordan, do you like me?' Or maybe 'Jordan, the girls in my bunk think you like me.' Then if he laughs in your face, you know it's not true.*

But if he didn't laugh, what was she supposed to do? What if he got all mushy? What if he actually did want to kiss her—right then? What was she supposed to do? Fake a coughing fit and tell him she was super contagious? Run? Dig a hole and bury herself in it?

"What are you waiting for?" Jordan asked.

And for one crazy moment she thought he'd read

her mind. That he wanted to know why she was waiting to ask him the Question. But no. They'd reached the back of the mess hall where the kitchen was, and Jordan was crouched down with his fingers laced together. He was ready to boost her into the open window. That's the way they always got into the kitchen. He'd boost her though the window, then she'd unlock the door.

"Nothing," Priya answered. She stepped into Jordan's hands. Two seconds later, she was through the window and standing on the big wooden kitchen table. She leapt to the floor and hurried to let Jordan inside.

"I'm thinking hot for Joe tonight. Everything hot. Find the Tabasco for me, okay? And grab anything else you see that's tongue-burning," Jordan instructed, voice low.

Priya nodded. Oh, great. Now she'd lost the power to speak entirely. *Just do it. Do it, do it, DO IT*, she begged herself.

"JORDAN!" she practically shouted.

"Are you nuts? Do you want us to get caught?" he whispered.

"No," she whispered back. "I just wanted to ask—"

Jordan grabbed her arm. "Somebody's coming. Broom closet."

Priya reached the broom closet with two long steps. She jerked open the door and she and Jordan squeezed inside. He closed the door behind them just as the overhead kitchen lights clicked on.

Had whoever it was seen the closet door shut? Were they caught? All Priya could hear was her own heart banging away in her ears. She wasn't sure if she was near heart failure because she was afraid of getting sent to Dr. Steve's office, or because she and Jordan were as close together as two sticks of gum in a pack.

"I think we're safe," Jordan finally said.

*Speak for yourself,* Priya thought.

Jordan pushed the closet door open a crack, and Priya peered out. "Clear," she whispered. She scrambled out and hurried over to the cabinet that was the farthest away. "Tabasco," she muttered. "Tabasco, Tabasco."

"What did you want to ask me that was so important you almost got us busted?" Jordan asked.

Priya jumped. He was right behind her. She spun around to face him. "Um, I noticed that you got a makeover," she said. Which was lame. And not a question.

A flush started at the bottom of Jordan's neck and went all the way up to his forehead, with a stop to turn his ears into tomatoes. "So what?" he mumbled.

"Well, uh, some of the girls in my bunk thought maybe it was because you liked someone," Priya managed to spit out. She hoped her whole face wasn't as red as Jordan's ears, but she thought it was.

Jordan didn't answer.

But Priya had gotten this far. She wasn't taking silence for an answer. "So, are they right? Do you, um, liiiike someone?"

"Yeah," Jordan admitted. "I don't know if you need all that *iiii*. But yeah."

"Is it the person you keep staring at?" Priya asked. She couldn't ask if it was her. She just couldn't.

Not without barfing. "At the barbeque and tonight at dinner?"

"Yeah." Jordan ran his hands through his slicked back hair, eyes locked on Priya, waiting to see her reaction.

Alex was right. It was time for Priya to face the truth—Jordan liked her, liked her in a boy-girl way.

She felt as if a big chunk of earth was dropping out from under her feet. As if any second she was going to go into freefall. Jordan couldn't be her best friend if he liked her *that* way. And how was she going to survive without him?

What exactly was she supposed to do now?

chapter

"Up, up, up! Everybody up!" Grace exclaimed.

"We have ten more minutes," Gaby grumbled. "And I want to be asleep for all of them."

"It's the day of the D.C. trip, you guys!" Grace insisted. "How can you stay in bed?"

"I can't. I want to check my suitcase one more time to make sure I put in all the essentials," Valerie said, throwing off her covers.

"I thought you already packed everything you own. Plus some of my stuff," Sarah joked.

Priya sat up in her bunk and yawned. She'd slept for about five minutes. She'd spent the rest of the night trying to figure out how to deal with the Jordan crisis. And she still had no clue.

Becky stepped around from the sectioned-off area of the cabin where she and Sophie slept. "I see I'm not going to have to use my crowbar to get anyone out of bed today." She grinned. "Is something special happening?"

"D.C. trip!" Grace, Sarah, Abby, and

Valerie yelled.

"Woo-hoo!" Alex added.

"Oh, right," Becky said. "Speaking of the trip, here's the deal with the hotel. Our bunk is dividing into two rooms. Sarah, Brynn, Alex, Priya, and Valerie, you'll be in 704 with Sophie. And the rest of you will be next door in 706 with me. Everyone from camp will be on the same floor."

"Cool, we're going to rule the place!" Alex pumped her fist in the air.

"Yes, we are," Becky agreed. "But we're going to do it without disturbing the other guests." She glanced around the room, making sure to look every girl in the eye.

Priya didn't have to worry that. The only way she might disturb anybody is if one of the extreme challenges accidentally got a little loud. But there wouldn't be any challenges on the trip unless she could somehow figure out a way to make everything normal with Jordan again.

"You should all have signed up for your activity choices by now," Becky continued. "Some of the activities have tour guides, but guides or not, there will always be at least two Lakeview chaperones with every group. Sometimes you might have me or Soph, but if not, there will always be someone from camp with you if you have any problems. I don't have to tell you to listen to them like you listen to me."

"And maybe a little better than you listen to me!" Sophie added as she joined the group.

"So, it's breakfast, then bus—" Becky began.

"Then Washington, D.C., here we come!" Valerie yelled.

Priya had been looking forward to this trip since the minute it had been announced. But now when she thought about D.C., she thought about a situation she had no idea how to deal with. A big, icky, and, yeah, scary situation.

▲ ▲ ▲

Priya climbed on the bus. The bus to the big icky scary.

Her mother was big on self-help books and Dr. Phil to help her deal with her problems. Priya didn't have any self-help books on her, and Dr. Phil wasn't on the bus. But Natalie was, and Natalie had been going out with Simon since last summer. Two summers with the same boy. That had to make her a relationship expert, right?

Priya didn't know Natalie that well. But Priya was desperate. She rushed down the aisle, threw her backpack in the overhead rack, and threw herself down in the seat next to Nat.

"Hey, Priya," Natalie said, sounding a little confused. "Actually . . . I was kind of saving that seat for Simon."

"I know," Priya answered. "I mean, I figured. But I need help. I need you to be my Dr. Phil."

Natalie laughed. "Should I start pulling out a bunch of my hair? Or can I be your Dr. Phil without the almost-bald part?"

Priya forced herself to smile, even though

nothing seemed funny to her today. "All I need is the good advice part."

Simon headed toward them. "Can you find someplace else to sit—just for a little while? Priya and I need to talk," Natalie asked.

"Okay." Simon continued past them and grabbed a seat a couple rows back.

"Thanks," Priya said.

"Hey, I love to give advice. What's more fun?" Natalie joked. "It's a lot better than getting it. So what's the up?"

"The up is that Jordan wants me to be his girlfriend," Priya said, without taking a breath, without giving herself time to wimp out. "So what am I supposed to do?"

Natalie raised her eyebrows. "Well, what do you want to do? Do you want him for a boyfriend or—"

"No. No, no, no. Never in a million years," Priya interrupted. "He's like my brother. Almost."

Natalie held up both hands like a traffic cop signaling cars to a stop. "All righty then. Question answered. Now I have another one. Did he come right out and tell you he wanted to be your boyfriend?"

"Not exactly," Priya admitted. "I hinted around—'cause I had to, had to, had to know or I was going to go insane. And he hinted back. But it was totally clear."

"Totally clear hint. Mmm-hmm," Natalie repeated. "Did you hint that you wanted to be his girlfriend?"

"Wait, here he comes." Priya watched as Jordan headed toward them.

"Want me to save you a seat in the back?" Jordan asked her.

"No. Nat needs some advice. I better stay here," Priya said. She hoped that by the time Simon wanted his seat back, the seat next to Jordan would be filled. Then she could sit—anywhere that wasn't near Jordan. "Sorry," she mouthed to Natalie as Jordan walked away.

"So, did you give him any kind of indicator of how you felt?" Natalie asked when Jordan was out of earshot.

"I don't know." Priya frowned. "I tried not to give him any indicators of anything."

"Head count complete," Becky called.

"Let's roll," Evan, the counselor for Bunk 4D, told the bus driver.

The front door of the bus wheezed shut. It sounded like the bus was giving a huge sigh, the kind of sigh Priya felt like she had trapped inside her. "So what am I supposed to do now?" she urged Natalie.

"You've got to tell him the deal. Flat out. No hinting," Natalie answered firmly. "Jordan's your friend. You owe him that. Don't let him suffer."

Priya stood up. She realized she hadn't needed a self-help book. Or Dr. Phil. Or Natalie. She'd known what the right thing to do was all along. She just didn't want to do it. It was too hard.

But she would. Like Nat said, she owed Jordan the truth.

"So you'll do it, right?" Natalie looked Priya in the eye.

"Yes. Definitely. Just not on the bus. It's a conversation where you gotta have some privacy," Priya explained.

And a conversation where you needed some time to figure out exactly what to say. And even more time to find the guts to say it.

She shot a super-fast glance at the back of the bus. No open seats next to Jordan. Yes!

Priya spotted an empty place next to a cooler full of drinks. Perfect. She didn't want to talk right now. To anyone.

"Don't you think it's weird that they call it a mall?" Priya asked Jordan as they pedaled their mountain bikes down the trail that ran beside the Potomac River. "I don't see one Cinnabon place or a multiplex or anything."

She knew she shouldn't be rambling about proper word usage or whatever. But she didn't think she should tell Jordan that she didn't *like him* like him while he was on a moving bike. He might crash. He was wearing a helmet. Everyone on the Sites on Bikes tour had to wear a helmet. But still . . .

"Yeah. Mall. That's weird," Jordan answered, without looking at her. Not like you usually looked at the person you were talking to when you were riding bikes. But he hadn't looked at her when they were picking out the bikes and putting on the safety gear, either. He'd mostly talked to the ground.

Priya and Jordan pedaled in silence for a few

moments. She wished they'd stop somewhere, so she could just tell him and get it over with. This was worse than waiting to get a cavity filled.

"Three points if you sit on Lincoln's lap when we get to the memorial," Jordan burst out.

Hey! That was so the old Jordan. Even though the boy on the mountain bike next to her looked like the new Jordan. Well, except for the shoes. He was wearing his old sneakers for the bike ride, although they looked a lot cleaner than usual. Priya thought he might have actually used shoe polish on the white parts. Shoe polish. On sneakers. That was so wrong.

Priya shook her head. "Can't. Becky would probably lock me in the bus until it was time to go back to camp if I tried scaling Lincoln."

"First stop, coming up," their tour guide, Amber, called out. "Park your bikes in front of the steps of the Lincoln Memorial." Sophie and Kenny, the counselors chaperoning the trip, repeated the info until they were sure all the campers who'd signed up for the tour heard it.

"We won't be able to get off our bikes at every monument and memorial in the Mall," Amber said when she had the group gathered around her, "but you need to pay a visit to Mr. Lincoln. Let me tell you a little bit about the memorial before you go up."

Amber swept her arm out, grinning proudly, like she had sculpted the marble statue of the president herself. "Henry Bacon, the New York architect who designed the memorial, modeled the building that surrounds the statue after a Greek temple. There are thirty-six columns, one for each state that was in the Union when Lincoln died. Parts of the memorial are made from limestone from Indiana, granite from Massachusetts, and marble from Colorado, Tennessee, Georgia, and Alabama. Using materials from all these different parts of the country symbolizes Lincoln's preservation of the Union by bringing together resources from the North, South, East, and West."

The tour guide kept talking. But even though the facts were pretty cool, Priya couldn't pay attention. It was time to step up. She hadn't wanted to tell Jordan how she felt when they were on the bus. Or while he was operating a bike. But there was no reason not to tell him while they climbed up the stairs to the memorial. It wouldn't be that hard to make sure no one was listening. And even though the steps were big and made of stone, it's not like Jordan was going to be so shocked that he was going to lose control of his feet and go falling down them. *Plus, Honest Abe would want me to do it here*, Priya thought. *'Cause of the Honest part.*

Jordan waved one hand in front of Priya's face. "You waiting for Abe to send down an invitation?"

Uh-oh. Priya realized that Amber had wrapped up her spiel. "Nope, not waiting for anything," she told Jordan. "Let's go."

Everyone else was already climbing, except Amber, Sophie, and Kenny, who were staying behind to guard the bikes. *This is good*, Priya told herself. *It's the perfect time to tell Jordan how I feel without anybody from camp eavesdripping.* That's what her aunt always called it—dripping. It sounded a lot nastier than dropping, somehow.

"I keep thinking about . . . about what we were talking about last night in the kitchen," Priya said as they started up the stairs. "About the liiiiking. Maybe without all the *iiii.*"

"I keep thinking about it, too," Jordan admitted, eyes on the steps, as if he was talking to them. "It's all I think about." He finally looked up and pointed at her. "Don't laugh."

"I'm not laughing," Priya promised. She *so* wasn't laughing.

"There's something I have to ask you," Jordan said, eyes on hers.

Oh, no. Oh, no, no, no. She couldn't let him. He was going to ask her to be his girlfriend. And that was going to make it so much worse for both of them.

"Wait. I have to tell you something first," Priya nearly shouted. "I—"

"Too bad. I started first," Jordan interrupted. "Will you help me get Brynn to be my girlfriend?"

Priya stumbled, almost fell off the step and onto the one below it.

*Wh-what?*

Brynn? He liked *Brynn?* This wasn't the conversation she'd prepared for. Priya felt as if the neurons in her brain were overheating and sending out garbled messages. Brynn? Had he said *Brynn?*

"Brynn?" she asked.

"Yeah." Jordan's eyebrows came together. "What? You don't like her?"

This conversation was so out of control. "No.

Yeah. Sure. I like her."

"So, come on. Help me," Jordan said.

"How?" Priya's brain continued its meltdown.

"Talk to her for me. Tell her I like her. Tell her that I think she's pretty," Jordan answered in a rush.

Priya didn't think she could. How could she tell Brynn anything? Priya now had a puddle of goo inside her skull instead of a brain.

▲ ▲ ▲

Priya concentrated on pumping her legs and watching where she was going. That's about all she could handle right now. That was all the goo could handle.

Amber called for another stop at the Vietnam Veterans Memorial. She started talking about how there were three separate parts to the memorial—the wall, the statue of the three service men, and—

Jordan started whispering to Priya before she could hear the rest. "I changed my mind. Don't tell Brynn that I like her or that I want her for a girlfriend, okay?" He rubbed his hands on his khakis and streaks of sweat came off on the tan cloth. "Just find out what she wants in a boyfriend, okay? That would really help, because I've never, you know, liked a girl before. And I don't know what I'm doing, okay?"

What could Priya say? The guy was still her best friend. "Okay," she whispered back.

# chapter FIVE

Brynn gave a double bounce on the big bed closest to the window. It was hard enough to make Alex, who was lounging on the bed, bounce, too. "This mattress is a billion times softer than the ones at camp," Brynn declared. "It's going to be like sleeping in heaven!"

"Sleeping in heaven—wouldn't that mean you're dead?" Valerie asked from the other double bed in the hotel room that she was sharing with Sarah. Priya and Sophie had gotten stuck with the rollaways. Sophie had volunteered. She probably figured as a CIT she should set a good example. Priya had lost a marathon game of rock, paper, scissors. She didn't really care. Lots of times she and Sam—and sometimes Jordan—camped out in the backyard or just in the living room after watching scary movies. She was used to a sleeping bag with *no* mattress.

"Who cares?" Brynn gave another bounce as she answered Val. "Who cares if I'm dead when I'm this comfy-cozy?"

Priya looked at her. The girl Jordan liked. How had it even happened? He didn't even know Brynn, really. Was it her red hair? Or her green eyes? Or was it the way she sang? Or the way she somehow *made* you look at her when she was onstage? How did it happen to Jordan? Did he just wake up one day and feel it? Or did it happen a little at a time?

Val stood up. "Well, Brynn, if you're dead and all—" She backed up a step, moving toward the bathroom door. "Then you won't care—" Another step. "If I take the first turn in the big—" Another step. "Non-mildewish—" Another step. "Lots of hot water—" Another step.

Brynn hurled herself off the bed and raced toward the bathroom. But it was too late. Val spun around, whipped open the bathroom door, and darted inside. "Non-shower bathtub!" she cried as she slammed the door shut behind her.

Priya laughed. She couldn't help herself. Brynn grabbed a pillow off Valerie's bed and threw it at the bathroom door. "That was very sneaky!" she complained.

"You can use some of the bubble bath I stashed in there, Val," Sophie called as the sound of running water came from the bathroom. "Note I said *some*. Not all," she teased. "You can all use some," Sophie added. "It's yummy. Coconut and mango."

"I wonder who got the first bath in the other 4C room," Alex said.

"Gaby probably pouted until she did," Sarah answered.

"And the rest of them were probably happy to get rid of her for a while," Priya added, trying to sound normal. Trying to *participate*. She didn't want to have everyone asking her what was wrong. Not that anything was wrong. Except that if Jordan and Brynn became boyfriend and girlfriend, Priya would probably never see him again.

Brynn would be the one Jordan spent all his camp free time with. And back at home, he'd probably be IMing her every second. That's what boy/girl pairs at her school seemed to do, anyway.

So that was it. Nothing big. Just the complete and total loss of her BBFF.

"Hey, let's check out the view. I bet the mall looks cool at night," Sophie said, probably because their CIT didn't want them to spend any more time dissing Gaby.

Brynn leaned over and pulled open the curtains. "Awesome. All the monuments are lit up."

"Is it just me, or does the Washington Monument change color?" Alex asked. "From light gray to dark gray, about a third of the way up."

"It does," Sophie answered. "Priya and I found out why on our Sites on Bikes tour this afternoon." She looked over at Priya with a tell-them expression. The thing was, Priya couldn't. Priya hadn't heard what the tour guide, Amber, had said about the Washington Monument. Basically from the moment Jordan dropped his confession bomb, all she'd heard when Amber opened her mouth was, "Jordan likes Brynn, Jordan likes Brynn, Jordan likes Brynn."

Priya realized Sophie was still looking at her. "Oh, uh, you tell them, Sophie. You tell stories better than me," she said quickly.

"It's not a big story or anything. But it's sort of interesting," Sophie said. "The quarry they were using to get granite for the Washington Monument ran out, and they couldn't get an exact match. That's why it's two different colors of gray."

"This coconut-mango stuff is amazing. It's like I'm taking a bath in warm fruit punch. But in a good way," Valerie called from the bathroom.

"Fine. Gloat. Go ahead," Brynn called back.

"What did you three do while we were biking?" Sophie asked Alex, Sarah, and Brynn.

"We were in the group that observed part of a session of the Supreme Court," Sarah answered. "How completely cool is that? Just standing in the room. It gave me shivers." She smiled. "Oh, wait. I forgot." She pointed at Brynn. "That one's the drama queen." She pointed at Priya. "That one's the tomboy. I'm the— hmmm. At school, everyone would say I'm the bookish, quiet one, but at camp I'm the jock. Well, I'm one of the jocks."

"So you're a jook," Alex offered.

"A bock," Priya suggested, trying to think if there was any way to get this conversation around to boyfriends and what they should be like. She had to get a list out of Brynn. Somehow. And it's not like Priya had a lot of experience with conversations like that. Those were heart-to-heart girlfriend-to-girlfriend convos. She just didn't have those.

"Tell us more about the Supreme Court," Sophie urged.

"Wait. First you gotta tell us more about the Sites on Bikes," Brynn told her. She shot a sideways glance at Priya. "Was Jor-dan on the tour?"

"Why do you care?" Priya snapped, surprising herself. What was going on? Did Brynn already liiiike Jordan back?

*Makes your life easier if she does*, Priya told herself. *Makes your life suck if she does*, she couldn't stop herself from adding. There was definitely a little part of her—okay, maybe a not so little part—that was hoping Brynn would go "ewww, Jordan" when it finally came out that Jordan liked her. Because then Priya could have him back.

"Have you forgotten already?" Sarah asked. "Brynn's our drama queen. She's not happy unless there is some drama going on. She has no personal drama at the moment, so she's glomming on to yours."

"You're like our own little soap," Brynn told Priya. "We all saw the makeover. We all saw the staring."

The staring. The staring at *Brynn*. Suddenly, Priya got it. She just happened to be sitting next to Brynn at the campfire and that time in the mess hall when Jordan had been goggling. Jordan had never been staring at her. He'd been staring at *Brynn*.

And the burping. He hadn't wanted to burp at the campfire, because *Brynn* had said "gross" when she suggested it.

And the laughing. The laughing at that stupid "yummy in the tummy" thing Brynn had said. Priya should have known the truth right then. Right that second!

"Now we need the next episode." Brynn turned to Sophie. "So was Jordan on the Sites on Bikes thingie, as if we don't know? And was there more staring? Or more, you know, *more?*"

"He was there. And there was a little whispering between the two of them," Sophie admitted. "But that's all I'm saying." She stood up and knocked on the bathroom door. "I'm giving you another five to soak, Valerie."

"Whispering." Brynn opened her eyes wide in an exaggerated way, and Priya felt her neck get hot. She'd done more blushing in the past week than she had in the rest of her whole entire life.

*All right,* Priya told herself. *First thing I have to do is convince everyone that Jordan isn't crushing on me. It'll be easier to get the what-Brynn-wants-in-a-b.f. conversation going if I get that out of the way.* Priya hadn't told Jordan that pretty much everyone in her bunk had assumed he was crushing on her. Who needed that humiliation?

"Okay. You got me," she admitted to Brynn, her voice coming out louder than she'd planned. "Jordan and I were whispering. Do you want to know what we were whispering about?" She spread her arms out, including everyone in the question.

"I do!" Valerie scrambled out of the bathroom with a towel wrapped around herself. "I even got out of the tub early to hear!"

No one called dibs for the next bath. Everyone looked at Priya. "I told Jordan that all of you goofs think he likes me. But he said he doesn't. I mean, duh, he likes me. We're best friends. But I was right all along. He doesn't like me like that." Priya sucked in a huge breath. "Which is good. 'Cause he's not my type. Not what I'd want in a boyfriend at all. Uh, so what do you guys look for in a boyfriend?"

*Uh, so what do you guys look for in a boyfriend?* Geez. Totally lame. Totally awkward.

But at least she'd gotten something out. She'd made a start.

Yeah, she'd made a start at helping her best friend not be her best friend anymore. And why? Because for right now, she still *was* Jordan's best friend. So she had to do what he'd asked her to do.

"It's not like I was looking, because I wasn't. I was anti-looking," Sarah said. "But it's cool that David likes some of the same stuff I do. He's not as serious about softball as I am. But he'll play. And he's funny. He cracks me up. I like that."

Hey, it worked. She got an answer to the boy-friend question. *Score! My lose-a-friend plan is going great!* Priya looked over at Brynn.

"I definitely want a boy who likes what I like," Brynn said. "It would be so fun to go to *The Elephant and the Grapefruit* at the Kennedy Center tomorrow with a boy. I mean, I know it's a group thing. But it would be fun if there was a boy I was into. We could hold hands, and at intermission we could talk about what the play meant, and the performances and the costumes and the sets and everything."

*A boy who likes what she likes. Remember that,*

Priya thought.

*You're Jordan's friend. He wants this. Remember* that, she had to tell herself one second later.

"I'm still trying to wrap my noggin around Jordan saying he isn't ga-ga for you," Valerie told Priya. "Not that he would use the word ga-ga. But talk about liking the same things—you guys could be the same person. And Nat did say that Jordan was asking the other guys for girlfriend advice."

"Yeah, what about that? And the different clothes?" Alex said.

"Don't forget the hair!" Brynn added.

"Gotta be for someone else," Priya said. "He didn't tell me. I—I—" She shook her head. "We've always told each other everything since forever."

Her eyes began to burn. She couldn't believe this. She felt like she was about to cry. She never cried. The last time she'd cried was when Jordan had accidentally slammed her finger in a car door. And that was two years ago.

Priya blinked rapidly, praying no one noticed her wet eyes, and rushed on. "That's not even it. We've always just been there for every big thing, you know? Because we grew up next door to each other. So we didn't even have to tell each other stuff. We just automatically knew. I can't even believe that there's something he hasn't told me."

Man, why was she getting all emotional? Jordan *had* told her how he felt about Brynn.

But pretty soon there would be things he'd keep secret from her, wouldn't there? If he got a girlfriend, there would be things he'd only tell that girlfriend, right?

She sucked in a deep breath and tried to pull it together. "Whoever the girl is, it's not me. And like I said, I wouldn't want Jordan for a boyfriend, anyway. We're too much alike. It would be weird."

Priya turned to Valerie. "So what about you?" She scratched a mosquito bite on her ear and rushed on. "What do you want in a boyfriend?" She figured Brynn would keep saying boyfriend stuff if the group kept talking about boyfriends.

Valerie stared at Priya for a moment, then closed her eyes and thought. "Not much. Your basic gorgeous." She opened her eyes and pulled her pjs out of her suitcase. "Smart. Lets me boss him around," she added with a grin.

"Well, gorgeous. Who doesn't want gorgeous?" Brynn asked.

Valerie laughed. "We both have quite a list for two girls who haven't actually had actual boyfriends," she commented.

"Until a few weeks ago, I didn't even want one," Sarah said.

*So gorgeous goes on the list, too,* Priya thought. Was Jordan gorgeous? She'd never thought about it. He wasn't hideous or anything. He didn't have two heads. And anyway, there wasn't much he could do about that one way or the other.

"I'm not even sure I want a boyfriend yet," Alex began. "And I absolutely know my parents would freak at the idea."

"Oooh. And I want someone that listens when I talk. And someone who can dance," Brynn interrupted. "And who says I look nice when I dress up."

Priya's forehead wrinkled as she concentrated. She needed to remember all that until she met Jordan at eleven.

▲ ▲ ▲

Priya hit the button that illuminated the dial of her waterproof watch. The watch even had a compass. Not that she'd need one to get downstairs to the lobby.

Ten fifty-seven. Time to leave. It was a good thing she'd ended up on the rollaway. It made sneaking out easier. She sat up slowly and stripped off her pajamas. She had a t-shirt and a pair of shorts on underneath. Her flip-flops were positioned carefully at the side of the bed, ready for her feet.

She shot a glance around the room. Sophie had kicked off the covers, but she was still asleep. Everybody else was conked out, too. Priya slid her feet into the flops, wincing at the soft sound they made slapping against the carpet as she made her way toward the door. She paused long enough to grab the extra key card off the dresser. And she was outta there.

Priya felt like there was a mega-flashlight on her as she waited for the elevator. Every second, she expected somebody to ask her exactly what she was doing out in the hallway by herself in the middle of the night. She let out a breath she hadn't even known she was holding when the elevator gave a little *ping* and the door opened.

Jordan was already in the lobby when she got down there. "What did she say? What did you say? You didn't say I liked her, did you? You were just supposed to find out what kind of boyfriend she wants, not say I liked her," he blurted out, not bothering with a "hi" or anything.

"Get a grip, please," Priya told him. She silently told herself the same thing. She was going through with the lose-a-friend thing. If she didn't, she'd probably lose him anyway. But in a worse way.

Priya pushed Jordan toward a little padded bench that was out of the sight of the people at the reception desk. "Sit," she ordered. Jordan sat down and so did she.

*Is he gorgeous?* The thought just kind of exploded in her head. Jordan's eyes were this mossy green and—

Not important.

"What. Did. She. Say?" Jordan asked. The muscles in his neck were tight, and his teeth were almost clenched as he ground out the words.

"Here goes. The list. One—Brynn wants someone who likes what she likes," Priya began.

"Wait. What does she like?"

Priya thought for a second. "Plays. Everything about them. Being in them. Watching them. Reading them, I'm pretty sure. The backstage stuff. Everything," she said.

Jordan made a scooping "more, more" gesture with both hands. "Two—she wants a boyfriend who listens to what she says," Priya obediently continued.

"Three—she wants a boyfriend who tells her she looks nice when she dresses up. Four—" Priya hesitated.

"You didn't forget, did you?" Jordan clapped his hands on his head. "Tell me you didn't forget."

"I didn't forget. I might have the order messed up on some of these. Anyway. Four—she wants a good dancer. And five—she wants somebody gorgeous."

Jordan leaned over, elbows on his knees, and stared at the floor. "This is hopeless."

"That's kind of extreme," Priya said. He sounded so . . . defeated. So not Jordan. "I've seen you dance at socials. I've even danced with you. You're okay. So that's one off the list. And, hey, if this all works the way you want it to, maybe Brynn will go with you to the Potomac Cruise Dance. I heard some guys are asking girls."

He still looked like he'd been eating dirt or something. Just completely miserable. Priya had figured getting him Brynn's list would be all she'd have to do as Jordan's GBFF. Clearly not. Clearly he needed further assistance. *You can do this*, she told herself.

She knocked shoulders with him. "Now tell me I look pretty."

"Why?" He didn't look up.

*You don't think I do?* Priya felt like asking. Even though that was stupid. She hadn't even brushed her hair. And anyway, this wasn't about her.

"For practice. Brynn practice," Priya explained. "She wants someone who tells her she looks pretty when she dresses up. You want to be the kind of boy she wants as a boyfriend. So practice."

"You look pretty," he muttered, still staring at the floor.

"See, I don't think it works if you don't actually look at the person," Priya told him. "So raise your eyeballs up and tell me I look pretty. Wait. No. Tell me a reason I look pretty. Like my hair or my eyes or some baloney like that."

Jordan straightened up and turned toward her. Man, his eyelashes were long.

"Your eyes are almost the same color as my dog's," Jordan told her.

Priya tried to imagine how Brynn would feel about hearing that. She shook her head. "I'm not an expert. But comparing a girl to a dog . . . probably not a great idea."

"But Dodger's eyes are this amazing brown-gold. They're really pretty," Jordan protested.

"I know. I've seen them up very close—with slobber dripping down on me. But probably go with something more normal. You could just say 'I like your dress' or something," Priya said.

Jordan nodded. "I can do that."

"Yes, you can, my friend! So two down. And listening to her—that's easy. So you got three." Priya counted on her fingers. "And I think you're—" *Gorgeous.* The word almost slipped out. Where had *that* come from? "I think you're decent in the looks department. So that just leaves liking what she likes."

"So I need to go to the play tomorrow."

"Instead of the Air and Space Museum?" Priya blurted out. "We have the whole place mapped out. We know how long we're going to spend at each—" She forced herself to stop. *Best friend*, she reminded herself. *He's your best friend, so be his.*

She swallowed hard. "Going to the play is the perfect way to get Brynn interested in you." Priya stood up. "Come on. The hotel has computers for the guests. Let's go online and read some reviews of the play. We can find some smart stuff for you to say about it. 'Cause we both know you're not going to come up with anything out of your own head."

Jordan grinned. "Sweet."

Priya led the way to the small room near the reception counter. It was empty. Bonus.

"What's the name of the play again?" Jordan asked as he sat down in front of the nearest monitor.

"*The Elephant and the Grapefruit*," Priya answered.

Jordan Googled the play. Priya grabbed the computer next to his and Googled it, too. "You read the *Washington Post* review. I'll take the *New York Times*."

They read in silence for a few moments. "Do you know if the grapefruit is a person?" Jordan asked.

Priya laughed. "I'm pretty sure there isn't an elephant of any kind in the whole thing. It's symbolic. I think it might represent a country. Or maybe a circus."

"Or possibly people with big ears," Jordan suggested.

"Or big noses," Priya shot back.

"Or wrinkly skin." Jordan spun his chair around on its wheels. "That's it! I'm a genius. Grapefruits have weird skin, too. Not wrinkly, but sort of, I don't know . . ."

"Almost pimply," Priya said.

"Yeah, or at least acne-pitted," Jordan answered. "That's it. We've cracked it. It's a play about the problems of bad skin."

*We're back. Me and Jordan. Jordan and me,* Priya thought. *But for how long?*

"You are a genius. And you know what else?" Priya asked. "Suddenly, I really want a candy bar. A big, chocolaty candy bar." Priya closed her eyes. "And maybe a bag of really greasy potato chips."

"So you're saying you want to join the people with bad skin. You want zits," Jordan teased. He grinned again. He looked extra cute when he grinned. *Wait. Where did that come from?* Priya thought.

"So many zits," Priya agreed, glad that Jordan couldn't really read her mind, even though sometimes it seemed like he could, in that best friend kind of way. "You want some, too? There's a vending machine."

"Get me a big bucketload of pimples with some blackheads on the side," Jordan told her, digging in his pockets for money. Then the smile slid off his face. "Better not," he said. "Gorgeous was on Brynn's list, remember?"

"Well, I'm still going," Priya said. "I'll get you some nice breath mints." *Oh, ewww. He better not use them for any kind of impressing-Brynn prep,* she thought. "I'll be back in a minute. Find something intelligent to say tomorrow. Because the horrors-of-bad-skin interpretation isn't going to cut it with Brynn."

Priya hurried toward the little alcove where she'd spotted the vending machine when they'd checked in. She hesitated when she felt something on the inside of her thigh. Something . . . drippy. Warm.

She spotted a ladies' room and made a detour. The pink and turquoise room was empty. Priya ducked into the closest of the three stalls, and got her shorts down as fast as she could. She perched on the edge of the toilet seat. Her stomach did a slow roll as she saw the streak of blood on her leg and the red stain on her underpants.

It took her a second to realize she'd gotten her period. Even though she'd had The Talk with her mom. And they'd discussed it in health class. And she and her bunkmakes had just been talking about period stuff during the "I Never" game.

But at first Priya had just thought—*something's wrong. Something's really wrong.*

Then it clicked, and she pulled her underwear to the side and checked her shorts. A couple of tiny spots of blood, but nothing that anyone would notice. Nothing *Jordan* would have noticed. Okay, okay. Good.

Her underwear was ruined. She had to toss it. But not until she got upstairs and put on a new pair. She'd find a bag and throw this pair away somewhere outside the hotel room so no one would see it in the bathroom trash. She didn't need everyone talking about her. Looking at her. She could deal with this on her own.

So, the first step in dealing was getting a pad. She couldn't just stay in the stall all night bleeding on herself. Priya cleaned herself up as well as she could with some toilet paper, then she hiked up her shorts and stepped out of the stall. There was no vending machine for pads. Great. Her mother had sent some stuff with her to camp—just in case. But Priya hadn't brought any of it on the trip.

She slammed the door stall door shut. *Toilet seat covers*, she decided. She could make a pad out of toilet seat covers. Priya pulled out about ten of the covers and folded them into a bulky rectangle. She got her shorts down again and positioned the "pad" in the center of her underpants, pulled them up, then her shorts.

It felt . . . like she had a huge wad of paper between her legs. But it was better than nothing. She waddled out of the stall and studied herself in the mirror. From the front she looked okay. From the back she looked a little bulky. Nothing anybody should notice, though.

She hurried out of the bathroom and toward the elevator, then stopped and rushed back to the computer room. "Uh, Jordan, I have to go. Keep reading the reviews. You'll find something good."

She backed out quickly, not wanting to give him the bulky view, just in case, not giving him time to answer.

"Hey, Priya, what's up?" he called after her.

She pretended she hadn't heard him. It's not like she could tell him. There were some things you just couldn't tell a boy. Even if he was the best friend you'd ever had.

chapter

# SIX

Priya opened the hotel room door and flipped off her flip-flops. It was almost impossible to tiptoe in flip-flops. She stepped inside, then quietly shut the door behind her. *Underwear*, she thought. *First, I need new underwear.*

Except even though her toilet-seat cover pad was ginormous, Priya was pretty sure she already felt a new wet spot. The thing just didn't fit right. Which meant her new underwear would get wrecked, too. And she could end up with blood on her pajamas. And maybe even on the hotel sheets.

She stood frozen in the dark room, feeling suddenly overwhelmed. What was she supposed to do?

Priya could wake up Sophie. But going to their CIT would make such a production of the whole thing. Not that Sophie wasn't cool, but . . .

Who else? Priya's eyes skimmed over the sleeping girls. She didn't know any of them well enough for something like this. Something this *personal.* Except in that "I Never" game they'd all talked about some personal stuff. Alex had admitted that she wanted to know if she was the only one who hadn't gotten her period. And Abby had said she was freaked about going to a doctor for not getting hers. That was totally personal information.

Priya was pretty sure Valerie had said she'd gotten her period during the game. And Val was in the bed closest to the door. And Priya needed help. So she tiptoed over.

"Val," she whispered.

"I didn't take the eyeball out," Val muttered, throwing one hand over her face.

"Valerie, wake up."

But it was Sarah who answered. "What's wrong?" She sat up and looked at Priya.

"Nothing." She'd been okay with telling one person. Just one. She'd been in a bunk with Valerie and everyone for half the summer, but she didn't know them that well.

Sarah yawned. "Nothing?" she sounded confused.

Why wouldn't she be? You didn't stand over somebody's bed in the middle of the night for nothing. *Spit it out,* Priya told herself. "Nothing, except I got my period. And they don't have a machine in the bathroom, and I don't have any stuff," she confessed.

"Oh, wow. Are you okay? Do you want me to wake up Sophie? Or I could run and get Becky," Sarah offered.

"No, that's okay, " Priya said quickly. "I just

wanted to borrow a pad."

"I don't have anything with me. I should, since who knows when mine will come back. But maybe Val does." Sarah grabbed Valerie by the shoulder and gave her a shake.

Val blinked rapidly, then stared around the room like she'd never seen it before. "D.C. field trip. Hotel," Sarah whispered, helping her out.

"I was having the freakiest dream." Valerie shook her head, like she was trying to shake the dream free. "What's going on?" she asked Sarah.

"Priya got her period! She needs to borrow some pads," Sarah explained. "And keep it down. Everybody else is still asleep."

"No prob," Val said. She flipped on to her stomach, leaned over the side of the bed, and pulled her suitcase out from underneath. Then she jerked upright. "Wait. You got your period? It's your first one, right? Are you okay?"

Priya wished Valerie would just hand over the pad so Priya could run into the bathroom. Why did other girls always want to talk about stuff so much?

"Are you getting food? Because if you are, you have to share," Brynn said softly from the other bed as Val leaned back down and started rooting through the suitcase.

"I wasn't. But—" She pulled a big bag of M&Ms out from a side pocket and tossed them to Priya. "If you're like me, you're jonesing for chocolate right now."

"I *so* am," Priya answered. "Is that a thing? I mean,

is that something that happens to you when you get it?"

"I love chocolate always," Valerie said. "But there are times when it is vital for my survival."

Priya ate a handful of the candy. Maybe the talking wasn't so bad if it came with M&Ms.

"Hey, I'm the one who asked for food," Brynn complained.

"Priya has priority. She got her period, so it's like a medical thing," Valerie answered.

"Should we try to find you a heating pad or something?" Brynn asked. "Maybe at the front desk?" She blinked. "Hey, wait. Didn't you say you never? During the game?"

"First time," Priya admitted.

"I read this cool thing. In Uganda when a girl gets her first period, she stays home from school, and her mom and aunts hang with her and fill her in on everything she needs to know," Valerie said. She pulled a little cloth pouch out of her suitcase and gave it to Priya. "Then later her girlfriends come over and party, and they sing this beautiful song about menstruation."

"I'll sing you a beautiful song about menstruation if you give me some of those M&Ms," Brynn offered. Priya popped another handful, then passed the bag. Then she hurried over to the rollaway and grabbed pajamas and clean underpants out of her suitcase.

"Be right back," she whispered, then locked herself into the bathroom.

A moment later there was a soft knock on the door. "It's Alex. I'm leaving some Midol from Val outside the door. It's good if you have cramps. Have you got them?"

Priya realized she did. She'd thought her tight achy stomach was from dealing with all the Jordan craziness.

"A little. Sorry I woke you up," Priya told her.

"I'm having some of my sugar-free Reese's I stashed away, so I'm not complaining," Alex answered.

"I'm leaving you the rest of the M&Ms." It was Brynn. "Well, the rest after this handful." She cleared her throat. Then she started to sing softly. Yes, sing. *"Priya, you're now a woman/ And that's sayin' somethin'/ You get free chocolate/ And that's saying a lot . . ."*

Priya started to giggle, her whole body shaking so hard she had trouble sticking the wingie things of the pad to her underpants.

"Why is everyone up?" she heard Sophie ask.

"We're celebrating Priya, the way they do in Uganda," Brynn answered. *"She's menstruating, so we're celebrating,"* she added in song.

"You okay in there, Priya?" Sophie was right outside the door now.

"Yeah," Priya answered.

The truth was, she was more than okay. She was good. Thanks to her roomies.

Her girlfriends.

How had she gotten along without girlfriends—real ones—before this summer? Boys were great. But boys would have been useless in this situation. Boys wouldn't have known she needed chocolate. Boys definitely wouldn't have been able to give her pads. And they wouldn't have made her laugh by singing to her about menstruating. They probably wouldn't even say the word 'menstruating.'

Sometimes you really just needed your girls around you.

Priya and Alex staggered off one of the National Air and Space Museum's flight simulators. It still felt kind of weird walking with a pad in her underwear. But at least she didn't have to waddle the way she had when she'd had all those toilet-seat covers stuffed down her underpants.

"How amazingly cool was that?" Alex asked.

"Extremely amazingly cool," Priya said. Her head felt like it was still somewhere around her toes after that last barrel roll they'd done. It had really felt like they were flying through the sky in one of those old-fashioned barnstormer planes, like the one Snoopy rode in when he was in Red Baron mode.

"Where to next?" Alex retucked her navy shirt into her shorts.

"Let's check the map," Priya answered. It was the map that she and Jordan had sent away for and used to plan out almost every minute of their trip to the museum. The place was massive. "Next up—the paper airplane contest in the How Things Fly gallery. I'm an expert at paper airplanes. I've had a lot of practice—I like to throw them at my little brother—and I can get some extreme distances."

"I only know how to do the basic," Alex admitted.

"I can teach you some variations, no prob." Priya lowered her voice. "I owe you for last night. Or we don't have to do the planes at all. I mean, we don't have to follow the schedule Jor—" She stopped. "The schedule I planned out."

"Are you kidding? It seems like you know more about this place than the tour guides. Can you believe Brynn attempted to talk me into going to that *Elephant and the Basketball* play with her instead of coming here? She's my best camp friend. And I'd do almost anything for her. But, puh-leaze."

"Grapefruit," Priya corrected automatically. She wondered how Jordan was doing. Only about the thousandth time she'd wondered the same thing since she hit the museum this a.m. Had he found the perfect thing to use to impress Brynn in one of the reviews after she'd bailed on him last night?

"Huh? Grapefruit?" Alex shook her head.

"The name of the play. *The Elephant and the Grapefruit.* Not basketball," Priya explained.

Priya suddenly felt like spewing the whole Jordan slash Brynn deal to Alex. That was what girlfriends did. Talked. And Alex was getting to be a girlfriend. Except it wasn't Priya's story to tell. It didn't have anything to do with her. So Jordan liiiiked Brynn and was going to try and get her to liiiiike him back today while they were at the play. What did that have to do with Priya? A big fat donut of nothing. So it's not like she'd be talking over a problem with Alex in a girlfriend kind of way. Because there was no problem.

So why did Priya have a kind of sick feeling in

her stomach?

It was just period cramps, she decided. That or a side-effect from the flight simulator. Or a combo of the two.

"How do you think the writer came up with that title?" Alex asked, pulling Priya out of her thoughts. "Come on. *The Elephant and the Grapefruit?*"

"*The Elephant and the Grapefruit* is the most fabulous thing I've ever seen," Brynn gushed as she, Sarah, and Val came into the hotel room after the play. "I want to be an actress more than ever. I can imagine myself up there on that stage in the Kennedy Center already, tears streaming down my face like in that scene with the basketball." Her eyes were moist, like she might start crying right then. And Jordan was crushing on her? Brynn was okay, nice even. Okay, she was actually cool last night. But wouldn't all the drama drive Jordan a little cuckoo?

"There was a basketball?" Alex exclaimed. "I'm psychic!"

"For you," Val said quietly. She passed Priya a piece of paper, then plopped down on her bed.

Priya opened the note and read it. *Meet me in the lobby. Now! Life and death!!—Jordan.* She sprang up from the rollaway and started toward the door. She had her hand on the doorknob before she thought of Sophie. Priya spun back to face the room chaperone. "Sophie, is it okay if I go down to the gift shop for a minute? I need to stock up on pads. I don't want to keep borrowing from everybody."

"Sure. Go ahead. I'll expect you back in fifteen," Sophie answered.

Priya raced back over to her bed, grabbed her wallet—to make her lie believable—and bolted before anyone could ask to go with her. She decided not to wait for the elevator. *Life and death*, her feet pounded out as she charged down the seven flights of stairs. *Life and death*. She flung open the door to the lobby and raced out. She spotted Jordan in front of the elevators.

*Is he going to be able to tell something is different with me?* The thought slipped in between all the worry about Jordan. *Is he going to know I got my period?*

*Doesn't matter. Life and death*, she told herself. "What?" she exclaimed as she raced over to him.

"I told Brynn I liked her dress," Jordan said. His voice sounded flat and dull.

"So?" Priya frowned. "How is that life and death?" She'd run down here ready to give him CPR or something.

"She wasn't wearing a dress," Jordan answered.

Oh, no! He was right! Brynn had been wearing pants and this shirt with big, full, lacy sleeves. "Well, okay, that was a mistake. But still not life or death, right?"

"I've hardly ever talked to her before. I've said 'hi.' And that was the first thing that came out of my mouth today." Jordan gave a low moan. "I sounded like a complete freak."

"She probably just thought it was funny," Priya said. She felt wetness drip into her pad, and she shifted her weight.

"I don't want her to think I'm funny. Not like that," Jordan shot back.

"Well, what about the play reviews you read? Did you try out something from one of those?" Priya asked, reminding herself to stay in Jordan's-best-friend mode, even though all she wanted to do was go upstairs and scarf down some more M&Ms.

Jordan gave a longer moan. "Yeah. Thanks for reminding me. I memorized this thing from *Variety*, and at intermission I told it to Brynn. Turns out she'd read the review. She knew that's what where I got it. So she thought I was this big fake who couldn't even come up with a thought of my own. She's never going to want to have anything to do with me now. 'Cause I'm a freak and a fake. And funny in the really bad way."

"You don't know that." Priya gave him one of their shoulder knocks. He didn't even smile.

"I *do* know that," Jordan insisted. "The counselors took the group to a food court after the play. I was already at a table with a couple of other people and Brynn was heading right toward me. Right toward me. And she veered. She *veered*, Priya."

The way he said "veered" made it sound like Brynn had grabbed a steak knife and stuck it in his heart. Repeatedly.

"I need some more help from you." Jordan started to pace. "You've got to help me turn this around with Brynn," he said as he passed her.

Priya started to get that sick feeling in her stomach again. It had to be from her period. It had been hours since the flight simulator. And she hadn't even taken the elevator. "How am I supposed to do that?" she asked.

Jordan stopped pacing right in front of her. He looked directly into her face, his mossy green eyes intense. "Can't you just . . . just tell her what a great guy I am? You know me better than anybody. Just explain that I'm not really a jerk. And then see if she'll go to that Potomac cruise with me. I heard a couple other guys already asked girls."

"I'll try." Priya's stomach gave a hard twist as she spoke the words.

▲ ▲ ▲

"Your sofa needs a little more padding." Brynn patted the edge of the bathtub where she and Priya sat side by side.

"I know. I just wanted to be able to talk to you without anyone listening," Priya explained. The chill of the porcelain soaked through the thin material of her shorts.

"Oh, goody. Secrets." Brynn clapped her hands. "About who?"

"About you, I guess. You and Jordan." Priya wished she'd bought some of her own Midol. These stomach cramps were killing her all of a sudden.

Brynn rolled her eyes. "Has Jordan been eating funny mushrooms in the nature shack or something? Because he was out of control at the play. He started talking about how it was all about acne."

*Thanks for not mentioning that detail, Jordan,* Priya

thought. "He was nervous. He really wanted to impress you, Brynn."

"Is that why he totally took credit for somebody else's review and made it sound like it was his own—before all the pimple talk?" Brynn picked up Sophie's bubble bath and took a whiff.

"Yeah. That's exactly why," Priya said. "Jordan doesn't know much about plays. But he knows you like them. And I told him you wanted a boyfriend who likes the same things you like—remember you said that the other night?" Priya didn't mention that she'd started the whole conversation just to get that info from Brynn. "He read a bunch of reviews last night so he could talk to you about the play today—the way you wanted a guy to be able to do."

"Oh. That's kind of . . ." Brynn let her words trail off as she fiddled with the top of the bubble bath.

"Flattering?" Priya suggested.

"Yeah," Brynn admitted. A little smile twitched at one corner of her mouth.

Priya rushed on. "You're probably thinking, what good is it to be flattered by a stupid freak boy who lies?" *Why did I say that?* she thought. *That wasn't exactly helpful.* "But that's not Jordan. I know him the way you know Alex. He's my best friend. So let me give you the skinny. You can trust Jordan. He knows all this embarrassing stuff about me, and he never blabs. And he's funny—not just in the dumb way, like about the zits. He's always making me laugh. And Sarah was saying that was important in a boyfriend, remember? And I think it's cool. Who doesn't like to laugh, right? He can make you laugh even if you're all upset about something."

Priya gulped, then continued. "And he'll try anything, as long as it doesn't involve eating weird food. I'm sure you could get him to go to another play or whatever. And he comes up with lots of fun games. He's fun. And maybe he's not totally gorgeous. But he is cute, right? I mean, I don't spend a lot of time thinking about cuteness. But his eyelashes are amazing. And his eyes are like moss—in a good way. And his freckles. I just like them. And he's a good dancer. Probably because he's really athletic. You want a guy who's a good dancer, you said so. You should go with him to the Potomac cruise. He wants you to. There's going to be dancing there, and you could see for yourself. Plus Jordan is really—"

"Stop! My ears are about to implode!" Brynn reached out and put her fingers over Priya's lips. "So, he's a great guy, that's what you're saying? Just nod yes or no."

Priya nodded yes. Jordan was the best. The absolute best.

"And if I gave him another chance, I'd probably like him," Brynn continued.

Priya nodded yes again. Harder. "And he likes you! I forgot to say that!" she burst out. "Jordan really, really likes you!"

*And I really, really like him!* Priya realized, horrified.

*He's the best.*
*And he's funny.*

*And he's fun.*

*And he's athletic.*

*And he's cute. With the eyelashes, and the freckles, and the moss green eyes.*

*And he's trustworthy.*

*He's just the best in every way.*

*And I completely, totally LIKE him like him,* Priya thought.

*I liiiiiiiiiiiiike him.*

"Then tell him I'll go to the Potomac cruise with him," Brynn said.

"O-okay," Priya answered.

*What did I do?* Priya silently wailed. *What did I just go and do?*

# chapter
# SEVEN

"Are you trying to kill me?" Jordan asked under his breath. "I gotta know the deal." He squeezed between Grace and Priya as the tour group gathered in the Pierce Mill the next morning. The mill was kept in the same condition it had been in in the 1820s. It couldn't actually grind grain anymore, but people were raising money to get it in working condition again.

"Shhh. The ranger's about to start the demonstration," Priya whispered.

She'd sat with Grace when the group took the Red Line subway over to Rock Creek Park where the mill was. Just because . . . well, just because she felt like hanging with Grace. Grace wasn't in the same room as Priya at the hotel, and Priya had . . . missed talking to her. 'Cause . . . 'cause Grace was funny.

And since she'd sat with Grace, it made sense to walk with Grace from the subway stop over to the mill. It would have been rude not to.

*Liar,* a little voice in Priya's head piped up. *You sat with Grace because you were too chicken to sit with*

*Jordan. And you hung with her on the way over to the mill so you could keep on avoiding him. Grace could have walked with Abby and Valerie—or a bunch of other people—if you'd met up with Jordan. She wouldn't have minded. And besides, when did you get to be all Miss Manners, anyway?*

Priya tried to ignore the little voice. She also tried to ignore Jordan, but she could hear him breathing next to her. It sounded like he'd been running, but she knew he hadn't. He was just all agitated because he wanted the scoop on how her convo with Brynn had gone last night. But Priya was kind of afraid to even look at Jordan, now that she knew she was in like with him. And if looking at him was scary—forget about talking to him. What if all her *like* just spilled out of her like a pile of those nauseating Valentine heart candies with the stupid sayings on them? LUV YOU. YOU'RE MINE. HUGS. So gross.

Jordan would flip. He didn't *like* like her. He *like* liked Brynn. And she had to tell him that Brynn *like* liked him. No. Not that. She had to tell him that Brynn was willing to give him another shot and go to the Potomac cruise with him tonight.

"Did you talk to her? Just tell me that," Jordan insisted.

Priya didn't answer. She kept her eyes on the ranger as he started the corn-shelling demo.

"Just tell me that," Jordan repeated.

Geez. Couldn't he wait a few seconds? Or a half an hour, or however long the ranger talk would take? Was the Brynn thing *that* important to Jordan? "Shhhh," Priya hissed at him through her clenched teeth.

"The guy's talking about getting corn off a corn-cob. Is this something you need to know in your life? I've seen you eat corn on the cob. You do it fine with your teeth," Jordan protested, not bothering to whisper or even use his indoor voice.

Her teeth. Had she brushed them well enough this morning? She didn't want to have any gunk in them when she talked to Jordan. Like he'd notice if she had a whole corncob in there. Not when he was thinking about *Bryyynnn*.

Kenny, the counselor chaperoning the tour, gave Jordan the death eye for talking during the ranger's speech. The ranger kept turning the crank on the spiked disk that scraped kernels off the ear of corn he was working on. "Using your teeth on other people's corn isn't that sanitary," he joked. "And I love corn so much, I'd end up eating it all if I tried to shell it that way."

Everybody laughed—even Kenny. Priya used the cover of the sound to answer Jordan's question. "I talked to her. Tell you when we get outside." She thought if she didn't give Jordan *something* right that second, he might explode. Or at least get in big trouble.

As the ranger finished up his ear of corn and started talking about the Industrial Revolution, Priya could practically feel volts of electric energy coming off Jordan. That's how stoked he was to hear what Brynn had told her. She touched the top of her head, checking to make sure her hair wasn't standing on end from the Jordan current. Nope.

But maybe she should have borrowed one of those sparkly barrettes Grace liked to wear. Not so Priya could keep her hair sticking to her scalp. Just 'cause the barrette thingies were pretty, and maybe Jordan would like them.

*Yeah, because Jordan's going to be putting a lot of thought into what your hair looks like while you tell him that Brynn's willing to go to the dance with him,* the annoying little voice commented. Priya tried to block it out, giving her hair a little fluff with her fingertips. It had seemed a little flat when she touched it before. She should have washed it last night, at least.

*Yeah, because Jordan would really notice if it was covered with three weeks worth of old, cold, stinky bacon grease while you're talking about Brynn,* that same annoying voice went on. Priya wished she could reach into her head, yank that voice out, and stomp on it. Instead she focused every molecule of her brain on the ranger. She asked four questions when he finished his talk. She would have asked four hundred more, anything to keep standing there in the mill where talking to Jordan wasn't an option. But Kenny said it was time to head back to the Red Line and move on to Fort Stevens, which was over in another section of the huge park.

Jordan managed to wait until Priya had taken one whole step outside the mill before he pounced. "Okay, you heard everything you could want to know about corn, and grinding, and factories. Now, please, just tell me what she said. Everything."

Priya forced herself to stop and turn and look at him, really look at him. Maybe she'd been delusional last night. Maybe she didn't liiiiike him. Maybe some of Jordan's like like insanity had rubbed off on her in some temporary way.

"What?" Jordan asked. "Oh, man, it's bad, isn't it? That's why you've been avoiding me and acting all freaky. It's really bad, right?"

Yeah, it was really bad. Those green eyes. Those freckles. And those memories of a zillion great times together. It wasn't temporary insanity. It was real. Priya really, really liked Jordan, with a capital L.

"Priya, you gotta tell me anyway," Jordan begged. "No matter what Brynn said. Even if she said that she'd rather eat dog poop than even look at me again."

"That's not what she said." Priya had to swallow hard to get enough saliva in her dry throat to allow her to continue speaking. "She said that she'll give you another chance. She said that she'll go to the dance with you tonight."

"Yes!" Jordan launched himself off the ground, thrusting one fist in the air. "I knew you could do it, Priya." He grinned at her. "I knew you could convince her for me. You're the best."

*Not true,* the horrible, way-too-honest little voice in Priya's head said. *Brynn's the best. That's what he really thinks.*

"So help me come up with a plan," Jordan said as they started walking across the park after the others. "I so need a plan. I can do okay with the dancing, I think, but what about the rest? If I open my mouth, I'm just gonna crash and burn like I did at the play if we don't figure out some strategy for me."

"Hey, I read some stuff about this fort we're going to. Sophie had some brochures," Priya answered.

"Lincoln watched a battle there. It's the only place one of our presidents was under fire while they were in office. Cool, huh?"

She knew she was babbling. But she couldn't talk Brynn-game-plan with Jordan. She felt like something might break inside her if she did. She'd told him what Brynn said. That was enough.

"What's your problem? Do you need more RAM?" Jordan asked.

*It doesn't matter if you help him or not,* the horrible, irritating, truthful voice said. *It's not like if he messes up with Brynn, he's going to decide he liiikes you. When Jordan looks at you, he sees a buddy. He might not even realize you're a girl. So why not help him out? Why should both of you be miserable?*

"RAM. Good one. Yeah, that must be it." Priya forced a laugh, feeling something crack beneath her ribs. "The planning turned out pretty bad last time. I think you should forget about a plan tonight."

"And do what?" Jordan's voice cracked.

"And just be . . . you. No memorized lines or anything," Priya answered. "The reason Brynn wants to go to the dance with you is because I told her what a great guy you are. I was talking about you. Not whoever that was that showed up at the play and spewed lines from some review."

"Just be me," Jordan repeated.

"Yeah. That'll work. Trust me," Priya said. *I totally know,* she added to herself.

"Thanks. You're the best bud ever!" Jordan slapped her on the shoulder.

That had to be the worst thing he'd ever said to her.

▲ ▲ ▲

"This outfit is so 'best bud ever,'" Priya muttered, staring at the t-shirt with the frogs on it and her best pair of jeans. Her top picks—only picks, really—for the cruise slash dance.

"What?" Sarah asked. She and Brynn were sharing the big mirror over the dresser, both putting on eye shadow, still in their bathrobes.

Priya shook her head. "Nothing."

"I can't wait to try swing dancing," Brynn said. "It always looks so fun in old movies. And Priya promised me Jordan is a good dancer."

Priya forced a smile onto her face. "Uh-huh."

"I'm going to dance with everyone," Valerie announced. "I decided if they don't ask me, I'm just going to ask them. A lot of boys are just too scared to ask. That's what my older brother told me, anyway."

"I'm more excited about the cruise part. I've never been on a cruise," Alex said. "It's going to be so cool out there on the river."

Priya watched Sarah use her little finger to smudge the eye shadow a little. At the beginning of the summer, Priya didn't think Sarah had ever worn any kind of makeup at all. But before the last camp social, a bunch of the girls had given her a makeover.

"You're getting good at that, Sars," Valerie commented. She sat cross-legged on her bed, twisting her cornrows into a wild little explosion on the top of her head.

Priya scooted over on the rollaway until she could see her face in the bottom corner of the mirror. How would she look post-makeover? Still "best bud"? Or someone Jordan could maybe . . .

Priya didn't let herself complete the thought. Jordan was all into Brynn. She knew that. But still . . . she wondered if the girls would do one for her. A makeover.

"Sarah, what color lipstick are you using?" The words felt bizarre coming out of Priya's mouth.

"Just Peachy," Sarah answered as she pulled the top off the tube. "You want to try it?"

"You do *know* Priya, don't you?" Brynn asked.

Sarah shrugged. "Just 'cause you don't wear makeup all the time doesn't mean you might not want to once in a while. I mean, I still don't wear it most of the time."

"My lips are kinda chapped, that's all," Priya answered.

"I have some Blistex you can use," Alex offered. She added another silicone wristband to her arm. She had on about seven now, all colors, with different words on each of them, like Truth, Peace, and Love. "Want it?" Alex held up the little Blistex tube.

Uh-oh. Why had Priya gone with that chapped lips fib?

"Ummm. Actually . . ." Priya began. "I thought maybe it would be fun. Just for a change. You know, because we're going to be on a boat and everything . . ."

Because we're going to be on a *boat*? What was

she saying?

Sarah looked over her shoulder at Priya. "It sounds like you're saying you want a makeover!"

Brynn whirled around. "Do you? 'Cause I'll do it! I love makeovers. And I'm good at it, right, Sars? Didn't David say you looked beautiful when I was finished with you?"

Sarah blushed a little. "Something like that," she admitted. "That was an amazing night. David held my hand and I got these hot shivers up my arm." She rolled her eyes. "I can't believe I said that out loud."

"See the results my work gets?" Brynn told Priya. "I'm a makeover goddess." She turned to Alex. "Call next door and have the rest of the bunk come over with all their makeup and whatever clothes they think might be good."

Priya felt like she'd just been strapped into the biggest, fastest rollercoaster ever built. And there was no getting off now.

Brynn sat down on the rollaway next to her and studied her face. "I don't think the peach lipstick is right for you. You need something a little darker. Like that deep pink you were wearing at the last bonfire, Val."

"Comin' at ya." Val launched a tube of lipstick at Brynn.

*That definitely isn't "best bud,"* Priya thought as she looked at the color. If Jordan saw her wearing it, he couldn't just see the girl who climbed trees and could burp the pledge of allegiance. Right? Would he even want to hold her hand—the way David had wanted to hold Sarah's?

*Brynn,* Priya reminded herself. *The girl sitting right next to you. Ring a bell?*

But it wasn't as if Brynn liked Jordan. She hardly knew him. Priya had had to work hard to convince Brynn that Jordan wasn't a complete idiot.

A double knock came at the hotel door. "Got it," Sophie called.

"I have the perfect top for Priya," Abby announced as she led the rest of the 4A girls inside. "It's brown, but it has these little tiny gold flecks."

"Perfect for your eyes, " Brynn told Priya, as she started to slide on a coat of the lipstick.

"And I brought a little glitter," Grace said.

"Glitter?" Priya exclaimed.

Brynn pulled the lipstick back. "Careful, or you're going to end up looking like a clown," she warned.

"Sorry, but glitter?" Priya protested.

"Not big specks. You can just put a little bit in your hair, and it will give it this shimmer," Grace explained.

"Best buds" definitely didn't wear glitter in their hair.

"Okay, bring it on," Priya declared.

Priya's stomach traveled up toward her throat as the elevator traveled down toward the lobby. Was Jordan already down there? What would he think when he saw her? Would he even recognize her?

She'd hardly recognized herself when she looked in the mirror one last time before she left the hotel room. The shirt and the caramel-colored eye shadow made her eyes look like there were flecks of gold in the brown. And there really were flecks of gold in her brown hair—gold glitter. Plus, she was wearing a skirt. A jeans skirt, but still.

The elevator came to a smooth stop. Priya was in the back, but it didn't take long for Abby, Grace, Sarah, and Candace to step out into the lobby. Priya sucked in a deep breath and followed them.

He was there. Jordan was there.

And he was looking at her.

And he was walking right toward her.

And he was smiling.

"You know who you look like?" he asked.

"Who?" Priya couldn't wait to hear this.

"That guy in the last Austin Powers movie. The one with the yellow hair who always wore gold clothes," Jordan joked.

Her heart skittered in her chest. She was not believing this. "You mean the guy who kept eating his own skin?"

"Yeah. That guy." Jordan flicked a speck of glitter off her shoulder. "Hey, is Brynn almost ready, do you think?"

It was like he'd punched her. Right in the gut. She couldn't pull in a breath. She couldn't breathe.

"Yeah. Almost," she managed to wheeze out. Then she turned away, so Jordan wouldn't see the pain on her face.

Not that he'd notice.

chapter

# EIGHT

"Hey, are you okay, glamour girl?" Grace asked as they started up the gangplank to the big cruise ship, its three wide deep blue stripes looking almost black in the twilight.

"Yeah. Fine," Priya answered. "Just need a bathroom, to, you know, check my pad." Clearly she hadn't been able to keep a basic normal human being expression on her face. Her period seemed the easiest thing to use as an excuse.

"Well, our boat is three stories, there's got to be a ladies' on there someplace," Grace said, as they stepped inside onto thick aqua carpet. "Want me to help you find it?"

"It's okay. I'll ask one of the ice-cream men." Priya gave Grace a little wave, then headed toward the closest guy in a white uniform and hat. He pointed her to a bathroom and she got herself inside as fast as she could without running. Her eyes started to burn the second the door swung shut behind her. At least she had the place to herself.

Priya leaned on the closest sink and stared

at herself in the mirror. "You are not going to cry. You are not a crier. You aren't going to cry now, because who knows what would happen to all this gunk on your face." She straightened up, and continued to lecture herself. "Jordan was just joking around. He doesn't really think you look like a psycho who eats his own flaky skin." She brushed a few specks of glitter off her neck. "He was just being funny. Like always."

The thing was, she didn't want him to treat her like always. That was the whole point. She's been turned into a complete 2.0 version of herself—with the slick stuff on her lips, and the sort of itchy stuff in her hair, and the pad between her legs, and the perfume Abby had sprayed on her. Couldn't Jordan see that she was totally different? So why was he treating her the same?

*Duh. Because all he can think about is Bryyyynnnnnn,* that horrible voice in her head volunteered.

Priya slammed out of the bathroom, hoping she had left the voice inside. "Sodas on the main deck," Abby called to her. "Come on."

"Okay." Priya obediently followed Abby out on deck. Her eyes immediately did a Jordan scan. She saw Brynn first. Brynn was smiling, smiling at Jordan. The be-yourself non-plan plan seemed to be working.

"Cramps?" Abby asked sympathetically.

"What?" Priya asked. "Oh, yeah. Yeah. Bad ones."

"I use this stuff called Flying Fox temple balm. You rub it on your temples and the inside of your wrists, or even right in the inside of your nose. It has all these essential oils that are mood soothers," Abby told her. "I'll give you some as soon as we get back to the hotel."

*By then I'll have to coat my entire body in the stuff,* Priya thought, shooting another glance at the smiling combo of Jordan and Brynn, even though she knew it was a very bad idea.

"You guys looked thirsty," Spence said as he came up to Priya and Abby. He held up two glasses of Coke and studied them like he'd never seen such things before. "They aren't bright red. And they can't be used as bug repellent. And I don't think Jenna has loaded them with salt or anything." Spence frowned at the sodas. "But I'm pretty sure you can drink this strange brown substance, anyway. I've heard people outside camp do."

"Thanks," Priya and Abby told him. Priya tried to remember if she'd ever talked to Spence—or if he'd ever talked to *her*—when they weren't playing Spoons. She didn't think so.

Priya heard Brynn laugh. She had this really loud, dramatic laugh. What was she laughing at? She didn't think Jordan was funny. She thought he was an idiot. Priya looked over at Jordan and Brynn, trying to look like she wasn't looking.

Abby elbowed her in the side. What? Was she being really obvious? "Spence was talking to you."

"Oh. Sorry." Priya grimaced as she forced herself to look at Spence. "What's up?"

"I, uh, I was just saying that one of the crew guys told me that those houses over there, generals live in all of them," Spence blurted. "It's called General's Row or something." He hurried away.

Abby shook her head. "That's not what he said.

He said he liked the, quote, shiny stuff in your hair, unquote. And you missed it. What were you thinking about, anyway?"

Brynn gave another look-at-me-I-should-be-on-stage trill of laughter. "Nothing," Priya said. She heard Jordan laugh back. "I was thinking about absolutely nothing."

Priya sat down at the table that was the farthest away from the one Jordan and Brynn had picked. She wanted to stop staring at them like a stalker. She also wanted to be able to eat. Her stomach was growling, and she knew she wouldn't be able to choke down any of her food if the Happiest Couple in the World was on display.

The seat she'd chosen meant Gaby was across from her. But Priya could deal with some brattitude, no problem. David and Sarah were next to Gaby, and Marc, a guy from David's bunk, was next to David.

"Hey, guys, isn't this boat fab?" Valerie asked, as she sat down at the table with Scott, a boy who was in this nature session with Priya and Jordan. Just thinking about Jordan got Priya twisting her head around and straining to see him. Yeah, he still looked like he was having fun. She turned back to face her own group, but all she could think about was Jordan and Brynn. Brynn and Jordan. What were they talking about over there? They didn't like any of the same things. Jordan couldn't talk about theater stuff—he'd already proved that. And Brynn couldn't—

Valerie nudged Priya. "Huh?" Priya asked.

"Scott was asking you something about fantasy football," Val said. "I know fantasy football doesn't involve leprechauns, but that's about the extent of my knowledge, so I can't answer for you."

"Sorry, sorry," Priya said. How many times was she going to have to apologize tonight? "What did you say?"

"I was asking what you thought of Eric Johnson for tight end," Scott said.

Priya shook her head. "You gamble on him, you better have backup. The guy gets injured climbing out of bed."

"Who do you like for backup?" Scott asked, leaning across Valerie. "It's looking like for Week 1 my options are going to be Courtney Anderson, Jeb Putzier, or Stephen Alexander."

"I'd go with Anderson." Priya pushed her hair away from her face, and felt a little glitter come off on her fingers. "He's big and has good hands. Plus, he's seasoned. The guy has no excuses for not producing."

"Cool. Thanks. I like that gold stuff in your hair," he added, before he leaned back.

"You are such boy bait tonight," Val whispered in Priya's ear. "Tomboy on the inside, glamstress on the outside."

"Hey, Priya," Marc said from across the table. "You know how we're having those swing dance lessons and that competition after dinner?"

"Uh-huh," she answered. Wait. Was that Brynn laughing? Again?

"Well, I wanted to know if you wanted to team up with me?" Marc asked.

Valerie grinned at Priya. "See, that's what I'm sayin'."

*That* is *Brynn laughing*, Priya decided.

Marc twisted his napkin into a ball. "So do you want to do the dance thing with me?"

Val nudged Priya again.

Priya blinked. "Yeah, sure. Sounds like fun," she told Marc.

*Like* anything *tonight is going to be fun*, that horrible voice in her head commented.

Priya grinned at Marc as she rocked back on her left foot. She wanted to look like she was having fun. Because Jordan and Brynn were only a few feet away. And they really were having fun. And she didn't want them to think she wasn't. Not that either of them was looking at her or anything.

"One-and-two, three-and-four, five, six," Marc muttered, staring down at his feet. His hand was sweaty in hers. The guy was trying so hard. He was so serious about it all.

"Maybe stop counting," Priya suggested. "Just listen to the music. It basically counts for you."

"But the teachers—one-and-two—said to—three-and-four—count—five, six," Marc said, still looking at his feet.

Out of the corner of her eye, Priya saw Jordan and Brynn do the cuddle step, where they ended up side by side instead of facing each other. Priya wanted to try that! But she and Marc so weren't there yet.

"I know, I know," Priya answered. "It's just that sometimes concentrating too hard can mess you up. That's happened to me in basketball. If I have everything the coach has told me running through my head when I'm trying to play, it can make me freeze up."

Marc nodded, but he kept on counting.

"At least try looking away from your feet," Priya suggested. "The teachers said not to look at our feet."

That got him. Marc immediately lifted his eyes—and stepped on Priya's toe. "Why don't we take a break? Hydrate," Priya said. She led the way to the drinks, which meant passing right by the Happiest Couple Ever.

Brynn whooped as Jordan swung her up to his left side, then his right. They kept on dancing without missing a beat. Or counting.

*Why can't I be dancing with Jordan?* she thought.

chapter

# NINE

"Okay, fifteen minute break, kitty-cats," one of the dance instructors called when the music stopped. "Then it's back here for the big dance-off. We have some cool prizes, so be ready to show your stuff."

Priya and Marc clapped along with the rest of the group. Then Priya noticed Brynn heading for the bathroom. And Jordan heading for the deck. They were going to be apart for the first time that night.

"I need to hit the ladies' room," Priya told Marc. "Meet you back here for the contest." She rushed after Jordan without waiting for an answer. But she hesitated when she stepped out onto the deck and saw Jordan leaning on the rail. What was she supposed to say? Was it okay to just go over there? She stood there for a few minutes, just watching him.

*He's still your friend*, she finally told herself.

"You were looking pretty slick out there," she commented as she stepped up beside him.

"I didn't think I'd like that kind of dancing, but it was fun. Almost like gymnastics or something," Jordan answered, all hyped up. "Brynn was really into it. But she likes dancing and singing and all that." He paused and looked over at Priya. "Thanks again for fixing things with Brynn."

Priya nodded. She couldn't talk. She suddenly felt like she had that day way back at Holly Perry's birthday party when she'd chugged all that lemonade. So cold inside. Like she had an ice-cream headache all over her body.

She cleared her throat. "Um, Jordan, I don't want to tell you this. But I think I should." The words came up out of that cold, dark place inside her.

His mossy green eyes darkened. "What?"

Priya cleared her throat again. It was like there was something in there that didn't want to let the words come out. "I saw Brynn when I was coming out here. She was talking to some other girls . . . she was talking about you, Jordan." She looked down. She shouldn't be doing this. But she had to. She couldn't lose Jordan to Brynn. Not now. Not now that Priya knew how she really felt about him.

"What did she say?" Jordan's voice was tense. Like his vocal cords had been tightened and tightened and tightened until they were about to snap. "It was bad, wasn't it?"

"She said . . . look, she was basically making fun of you," Priya revealed, and the words felt like they were cutting into her tongue.

Jordan took a step closer to her. "I need to know

exactly what she said. If you're my friend, you'll tell me."

There was no going back. Not now. "She was telling the story about how you pretended the quote from that play review was something you thought up. She was laughing because it was so obvious you weren't smart enough to understand anything about theater by yourself."

"But why did she even come to the dance with me if that's how she felt?" The reflection of the lights strung around the ship's railing glittered in Jordan's eyes.

He wasn't about to cry, was he? No way. Jordan didn't cry.

"She kinda talked about that." Priya's brain raced as she tried to come up with an answer that made sense. "Brynn said she thought it might be fun to hang with somebody so totally different from her. But . . . but she said it was taking all her acting ability to pretend like she was having a good time."

Jordan leaned back over the rail. Far over. Like he was going to puke or something.

*Look at what you did to him,* that little voice in her head cried. *Look. At. What. You. Did. To. Jordan.*

*And to Brynn,* the little voice added. *Who was becoming your friend. One of your first girl friends.*

Priya slammed a solid lead gate down between that voice and the rest of her brain. She wasn't going to listen to that voice anymore. She couldn't. She was just doing what she had to do. She couldn't lose Jordan. That was that. He hardly knew Brynn. He couldn't be all that hurt.

"I'm sorry," Priya said. "Sorry I had to tell you that."

"It's not your fault." Jordan straightened up.

The little voice tried to say something from behind the gate, but Priya refused to listen.

"Hey, you two!" a voice called. Priya knew it was Brynn without turning around. She could tell Jordan did, too. His hands tightened on the ship's railing. "Ready to get back in there and cut a rug?"

Jordan grabbed Priya's hand and turned to face Brynn. "Priya and I decided to enter the contest together," he announced. "I'm sure you can find somebody else to dance with." He rushed Priya across the deck. "You look really pretty," he said loudly to Priya. "That stuff you're wearing on your eyes makes them look super golden brown."

Super golden brown. *That* didn't sound "best bud." Priya smiled. It felt like she was smiling everywhere. In her stomach. In her toes. In her super golden brown eyes. She was just one huge smile.

Until she saw Marc waiting for her. "Just give me one sec," she told Jordan.

She hurried across the room to Marc. "You know Jordan, right?" she asked.

"Yeah." Marc's eyes moved to Jordan, then back to Priya.

"Here's the deal. He came to the dance with this girl, and she just kind of dumped him. I'm his best friend and he needs me. Do you think you could find somebody else to dance with in the contest?" *Say yes,* she thought. *Please, please, say yes.*

"I guess," he told her.

"Great!" She realized she probably sounded obnoxiously happy. "I mean, thanks. Jordan needs a friend right now."

Priya spun around and flew back across the room to Jordan. She reached him just as the lights started to flick on and off. "Okay, gang. Time to start the contest," one of the instructors called. "Just keep on swingin' until one of us taps you on the shoulder. Good luck!"

And then she was dancing with Jordan. It was like playing basketball. Or swimming. Her body just knew what to do. Spin out. Spin back. Spin under his arm. Rock back. Let him swing her up to his right side. Then his left. Whee!

It was the best. The absolute best. Jordan was smiling at her. She was flying.

The crowd around them got thinner and thinner, as more and more pairs were eliminated. Jordan and Priya owned the floor. They covered the length of it as they danced. "Woo-hoo! This is awe—"

The words dried up in Priya's mouth as she caught a glimpse of Brynn standing in the sidelines. Her eyes were locked on Jordan. She looked so confused. So hurt.

Jordan grabbed Priya in another lift. She looked down at his face. He wasn't having any fun. He was faking it. Why hadn't she noticed that before? She was his best friend. She should have noticed in about a second and a half.

Priya sat next to Jordan on the bus back to camp. Because he was her best friend, right? And that's what you did—you sat next to your best friend.

Of course, Jordan didn't know he shouldn't be *her* best friend anymore. He didn't know he should hate her.

Brynn didn't know she should hate Priya, either. She probably wasn't thrilled Priya was sitting next to Jordan. Not after the way Jordan had slammed Brynn last night. But if Brynn was hating anybody today, it was Jordan.

Jordan, who was staring out the window. Looking like someone had just made him eat a whole bucket full of mixed-together food.

"I think I'm going to write Sam," she said. Because she couldn't stand looking at him, knowing she had made him so totally miserable.

"Kay," he said, without turning toward her.

Dear Sam,

I'm writing this on the bus back to camp after the D.C. trip. D.C. was cool. Jordan and I did the Sites on Bikes tour. It's weird. It was only a few days ago, but I can't even remember that much. Don't tell Mom. She'd freak about me not taking advantage of my enriching experience.

The National Air and Space Museum was cool, too. I entered this paper airplane contest. Mine went second-farthest. But, I don't know. Maybe I'm getting too old for paper airplanes or something.

Jordan and I won a swing dance competition. Woo-hoo! The prize was a bunch of CDs. Jordan let me have them all. I think I'll give them to Dad for his birthday.

Can't wait to see you, Sam. I'm kind of ready to come home. Camp's good, but . . . I guess it's kind of like been there/done that, you know? Or maybe I just have the flu or something. I'll get over it.

Hope you're having a great summer.
Bye!
Priya

chapter TEN

"Sleepyhead, it's time for dinner," Grace called. "You don't want to miss the taco casserole, *amiga. Muy,* well, I can't say *muy bien. Muy* fair semblance of food."

Priya opened her eyes slowly, even though she hadn't been asleep. She'd pretended to fall asleep the second they'd gotten back to the bunk. She'd also pretended to fall asleep on the bus, as soon as she'd finished writing that letter to her brother.

"Ah, she lives," Grace said, smiling down at her.

"She's alive," Candace echoed.

"Come on." Grace stuck out her hand and pulled Priya up from her bed. "What's the deal, too much dancing last night?"

Priya quickly looked around for Brynn, but she must have already left for the mess hall. "I guess."

"You guess," Valerie teased as she, Priya, Grace, and Candace headed out of the cabin.

"Come on. You and Jordan were the last ones on the floor. It takes a lot of energy to win first place."

"Right. You need to eat many servings of bad casserole to restore all those calories," Grace said. "You can have mine. I'm that much of a friend."

"Before we get with the whole group, can I ask what happened with Jordan and Brynn at the dance? I mean, they went together. And they were dancing together during the practice part. How'd you and Jordan end up as a pair in the contest?" Val asked.

"Yeah, you two were dancing together in the contest. How did that happen?" Candace asked.

Clearly, Brynn hadn't said anything. Maybe she was too confused. Or embarrassed. Or just too hurt.

"I don't know exactly. At the break, I went outside and I saw Jordan, and we were talking. Then Brynn came out, and Jordan told her that he was dancing with me in the contest." Priya shrugged. "I thought they must have had an argument or something. He didn't talk to me about it. We just . . . danced." She shrugged again. "He didn't talk about it on the bus, either. But I fell asleep kind of fast."

She'd wanted to be asleep. That's all she wanted. If she'd been asleep, then she would have been able to get away from herself for a little while. Priya just didn't want to be around Priya anymore. Who would? Who would want to be around a girl who'd treated her best friend the way she'd treated Jordan? She'd treated Brynn so badly, too. And Marc.

And now she was lying to even more people to cover up for what she did. Someday the whole stinking pile of badness might come crashing down on her. And maybe it should.

"Are you feeling bad about what you did?" Grace asked.

"What?" Priya exclaimed, her heart slamming into her ribs so hard it should have gotten splinters.

"About getting Brynn to go to the dance with Jordan," Grace explained as they headed into the mess hall. "You looked upset. I thought maybe you were thinking they wouldn't have gotten in that fight if you hadn't helped them hook up."

"You definitely shouldn't go there," Val said to Priya.

"No, you shouldn't. There's no way you could have known what was going to happen," Candace added.

*Yeah, there is. I made it happen,* Priya thought. She grabbed the closest empty seat at the Bunk 4C table— then realized too late that it was directly across from Brynn. Great.

"Why don't we go around the table and each say what our favorite part of the D.C. trip was," Becky suggested. "Since this is the first time we're all together— and awake—since we got back." She winked at Priya.

"I'll start," Abby volunteered. "There was this painting in the Smithsonian that . . ."

Priya whipped through memories of D.C. while Abby talked. The Sites on Bikes tour—where Jordan told her he liiiiked Brynn? No way. Helping Jordan research for his date with Brynn? Uh, no. The Air and Space Museum? Hanging out with Alex had been kinda fun. But the whole time Priya kept on thinking about how Jordan wasn't there. And where Jordan actually was. And who he was with instead of Priya. The cruise? Absolutely no way. She wished she could get a brain wipe of that night. Or at least of the part where she realized that Jordan, Brynn, and Marc were completely miserable because of her.

"Priya!" Sarah, Alex, and Abby called together with their hands cupped around their mouths.

She blinked.

"Your turn," Sarah told her.

"Oh." She hadn't thought of even one thing to say. Then she realized what the best part of the trip had been. "Okay, this might sound dumb, because it's not about D.C., exactly. At least not about any of the places we went there. But that night I got my period, and everybody in the room gave me stuff—Midol and chocolate and everything. And Brynn sang that song to me . . . that was the best. I guess 'cause I never really did the girlfriend thing before. Not like that, you know."

"Awww." Grace reached over and gave her a half hug.

"It was a good song," Brynn added with a little smile, but not her usual light-up-Broadway-all-the-way-from-camp one.

She didn't seem mad at Priya for the dance thing. Brynn must've thought the whole thing was Jordan's idea. *She must think he's a total psycho. With a cruel cherry on top. Which is so unfair,* Priya thought, her eyes going over to Jordan, even though she really didn't want to look at him. It hurt too much. In so many ways.

Yeah, like she expected, he was staring at Brynn.

Like he was wishing her head was plastic so he could look inside and just *understand.*

Sophie came by with a big pan of taco casserole and set it down in the middle of the table. Priya served herself a scoop. She picked up her fork, then looked over at Jordan again. He was still starting at Brynn.

Staring at Brynn. The way he had been at the campfire. The way he had been that other night at dinner. He liked Brynn so much.

*He asked for my help as his best friend. And I betrayed him,* Priya thought. There wasn't a worse thing she could have done. That was the lowest.

Priya dropped her fork and bolted to her feet. "I know I said it was going to be bad. But it's not going to be that bad," Grace joked.

"Oh, yes it is," Priya muttered. "It's going to be even worse." She looked over at Becky. "I need to take Jordan and Brynn outside for a minute."

"I'm sure it can wait until after—" Becky began.

"It can't. It really, really can't," Priya interrupted.

Becky met her gaze for a long moment. "Okay, but come right back in."

"Come on, Brynn," Priya ordered.

"I'm eating," Brynn protested.

Priya walked over, took Brynn by the arm, and led her over to Jordan's table. "We need you outside." She looked over at his counselor. "Becky said it would be okay. Just for a couple minutes."

"What are you doing?" Jordan asked as Priya tugged him up from his chair.

"I need to tell you both something," she answered

as she led them out the door. "Even if neither of you ever forgive me."

Priya released them outside the mess hall and forced herself to keep talking. "I lied to you yesterday," she told Jordan. "I didn't even see Brynn before I came out on deck. I didn't hear her say anything. She didn't say any of those mean things about you, Jordan."

"What?" Brynn and Jordan cried at the same time.

"What did you tell him I said?" Brynn demanded.

"Why?" Jordan burst out.

Priya looked over at Brynn. "I basically said you made fun of him, and that you were only acting like you were having fun dancing with him." She turned back to Jordan. "And I did it because . . ." She couldn't tell him. At least not all of it. "I did it because I was jealous."

"I can't believe I'm hearing this." Jordan stared at her like he'd never seen her before. Like she was something that disgusted him.

"You know how it is when someone, you know, liiiikes someone else. They want to spend all their time with them. It was already happening. You wanted to go to the play with Brynn instead of the museum with me, even though we'd been planning the museum trip since the beginning of summer." Priya reached for Jordan's arm. He jerked back before she could touch him. "I just didn't want to lose my best friend."

"Well, you did," Jordan told her. He took Brynn by the hand. "Let's go back in. There's nothing else to say to her."

And they left Priya standing there. Alone.

She couldn't follow them back inside. She'd die if she had to be in the same room with Jordan and Brynn for even one more second.

Priya raced off into the darkness.

Priya knew she couldn't sit in this stupid tree forever. All the counselors would have to look for her. Dr. Steve would have to call her parents. Everything would just be more of a disaster than it already was. Besides, she had to change her pad soon. Being a girl sucked sometimes.

She scrubbed her face with both hands, then slowly began to climb down, thinking about how fast she'd climbed up during that extreme challenge between her and Jordan. That wasn't even a month ago. It felt like about a billion years. Except when it felt like yesterday.

The walk back to the bunk was too short to come up with anything that felt even close to the right thing to say. Maybe because there wasn't anything. So all she said was "hi" when she stepped inside.

"Becky and Sophie are looking for you. I'll go find them and tell them you're back," Alex volunteered.

"I'll go with you," Grace said.

"Thanks." Priya walked over to her bunk and lay face down. No one said anything. The quiet felt like it actually had a weight, like it was pressing down on her, flattening out her lungs.

"So should we all throw pillows at her or what?" Valerie finally said. A couple girls laughed. Priya knew

Brynn wasn't one of them. Val stood up. "There's still a little free time. I'm gonna go to the rec room and, I don't know, play Sorry. Who wants to come?"

Less than a minute later the Bunk of Hideous Silence was empty except for Priya and Brynn. "Is it worth saying I'm sorry again?" Priya asked.

"Probably not," Brynn said. She sighed. "Jordan and I talked for a while after dinner. You were right. He really is a terrific guy."

Priya nodded. "I hope I didn't completely mess things up between you guys."

"I think we're going to be friends," Brynn answered. "But just friends."

Priya stared at her. "Why?"

"You know that hot shiver thing Sarah said she got when David held her hand?" Brynn plucked at her bedspread. "I didn't get that with Jordan."

"Oh." Priya thought for a minute. "Does he know?"

"Yeah, that's one of the things we talked about." Brynn picked up her pillow and tossed it lightly at Priya's head. "Now you've got to do it, too."

"What?" Priya cradled the pillow in her arms.

"Talk to Jordan."

Priya snorted. "Didn't I talk enough tonight? I doubt he ever wants to hear my voice again."

"You've got to tell him the truth," Brynn insisted.

"Wh-what?" Priya stared at her. Brynn raised her eyebrows. Priya nodded slowly. "Okay. I *like him* like him. But I didn't know at first. I didn't know until I was sitting in the bathroom with you telling you why you should give him another chance. And then it was too late. Well, it should have been too late. Then I turned into glitter-covered evil."

"Hey, I'm the drama queen, remember?" Brynn asked.

"So, do you forgive me?" Priya found it hard to ask the question, because she was afraid to hear the answer.

"On one condition. Make that two," Brynn said.

"Anything," Priya promised.

"First, give me back my pillow."

Priya smiled and tossed it to her. "That was easy."

Brynn smiled back. "Second, tell Jordan how you feel."

The smile slid off Priya's face. That was going to be almost impossible.

# chapter ELEVEN

Priya stretched out on a beach towel by the lake and closed her eyes. She was allowed to skip swimming today if she wanted to, because of her period. At least it would be gone soon.

And maybe she could use the time to finally get some sleep. Last night, she couldn't. Not even after she'd found Marc and apologized to him, too.

She kept thinking about what she'd promised Brynn. How was she possibly going to tell a boy who hated her that she liiiiked him? With all those *iiiis*?

She felt something wet on her forehead and brushed it away without bothering to open her eyes. Another wet drip. Then another. Had it started to rain? Priya cracked her eyelids—and saw Jordan standing over her in his bathing suit.

"Are you avoiding me now?" he demanded. "Because I'm the one who should be avoiding you. You're the one who acted like a butt."

"I'm not avoiding you," Priya said.

"Right. Keep on lying. You're getting good at it," Jordan shot back, his eyes narrow.

"I'm not lying." She was going to tell him the truth, the way Brynn wanted her to. But that didn't include spewing the fact that she had her period. You just didn't tell a boy you liiiiked that.

"You never skip swimming."

"Well, today I did. Deal with it." She locked eyes with him, willing Jordan to believe her. Finally, he turned around and started back toward the lake. "Wait!" Priya called.

"Why? Why should I?" But Jordan turned around and strode back over to her.

"I told you pretty much everything outside the mess hall, but I left something out," Priya began.

"Unbelievable." Jordan slapped his hands on his head. "What? Did you go to my house and pinch my dog?"

"No." Priya pulled in a long, shuddering breath. *Here goes, the absolute end of our friendship. Like it isn't pretty much dead already*, she thought. "Here's the deal. I was jealous, when I found out you liked Brynn."

Jordan rolled his eyes. "Yeah, you said that. Selfish much?"

"But it wasn't because we wouldn't be able to spend as much time together," Priya admitted. "When I was telling Brynn all the reasons she should want to go to the dance with you, I realized I wanted to go with you myself." She dug her fingers into the sand. They were shaking and she didn't want Jordan to see.

Her knees were shaking too, she realized. She

didn't think she'd be able to stand up if she wanted to. "But I didn't want to go with you as a friend," she continued, speaking to the tiny grains spilling across her hands. "I wanted to go with you as my boyfriend." She forced herself to look back up at Jordan, because since she was doing this, she should do it all the way.

He looked back at her, his face expressionless. Then he turned and walked away.

She thought it had hurt when she'd helped him prep to impress Brynn. But she hadn't known what pain was.

"Bye, Jordan," Priya whispered after him.

Priya caught up to Brynn on the way to the campfire that night. "I did it. I told him."

"So what happened?"

"He stared at me like this." Priya made her face a blank mask. "Then he walked away."

"Boys. Not so great with the communication skills," Brynn commented as they sat down on one of the dead logs around the fire.

"Thanks for making me do it, though," Priya said. "I probably would never have slept again for the rest of my life if I hadn't."

"That's what girlfriends are for, right? Making you do the things you don't want to do," Brynn said.

"I'm still trying to figure the girlfriend thing out," Priya admitted. "I mostly hang with boys. I mean, at camp I do stuff with whoever is in my bunk, but . . ."

"But no secrets or confessions or advice?" Brynn

started toasting herself a marshmallow.

"When I asked you guys what you thought it meant when Jordan brought up kissing—that was my first real girlfriend conversation, I think," Priya said.

"Hey, you made me a marshmallow for my s'more. How sweet," Grace said, plopping down next to Brynn and commandeering her marshmallow.

Priya laughed. "I'll make you one," she told Brynn.

"Later," Brynn said. "Jordan's coming over to talk to you."

"Maybe he wants to talk to *you*," Priya said, her heart starting to do an imitation of bumblebee wings.

"He's looking right at you," Brynn answered.

"Right at you," Grace agreed. "I'll sign an affidavit or whatever they're called." She moved down to the next log. So did Brynn. Priya started to move.

Brynn pointed at her. "Stay!" she ordered.

Priya stayed. She still owed Brynn . . . about a million. And if Jordan wanted to talk . . . well, she owed him about a billion, so she'd let him talk.

Jordan sat down next to her. But he didn't say anything. He stared straight ahead at the fire. Then he reached out and took her hand.

Oh, wow. Wow! Jordan was holding her hand.

Did that mean . . . ? It seemed like maybe her best friend wanted to be her boyfriend.

Priya stared straight ahead too. They looked into the fire without speaking. Priya's shoulders started to cramp up, but she was afraid to move. This was so . . .

It was so . . . strange. And there was no hot shiver. She shot a glance at Jordan out of the corner of her eye and caught him looking at her. It wasn't a lovey-dovey look. It was a this-is-strange look. Priya got a zap of best-friend telepathy. Jordan wasn't getting the hot shivers, either.

So . . . hmmm. What did that mean? Priya wished she could have a confab with all her new girlfriends. But she was pretty sure it meant that maybe Jordan wasn't meant to be her boyfriend after all. Maybe he was meant to be just her best friend.

Priya let go of his hand and gave a little shrug. Jordan gave a little shrug back. Then they both cracked up.

They were back!

Muscles loosened all over Priya's body. Muscles she hadn't even realized she'd been tensing.

This was . . . good. This was better than good. Like being best friends was better than anything.

"What were you doing holding my hand?" Priya joked. "I'm the nutso who thought I was in like with you. Not the other way around."

Jordan rolled his eyes. "I started thinking that if the only way I could stay friends with you was to be your boyfriend, I'd have to at least try it. Even if it was kind of insane."

"Which it was," Priya agreed. "Hey, you know today at the lake? When you thought I was avoiding you?"

Jordan's shoulders tightened up.

Priya lowered her voice. "I wasn't going in the water, because I have my period. It felt weird to tell you when I thought I was in like with you."

"Whoa. Too much information." He held up both hands.

"Wimp," Priya teased.

"That's not wimpy. No guys want to know that. Not just me," Jordan said.

Yeah, they were sooo back!

Priya pounded down the court, feinted left, then shot the ball to her right. She knew Jordan would be there. And he was. In the perfect position to take the shot. *Swish!* Beauty.

"That's the game, my friends," Jordan called. He slapped hands with Priya. "Nice one."

"Back at ya," she told him. "I have some contraband soda. Want to go sneak one? Maybe do some burping?"

"Nope. I'm meeting up with Brynn." Priya could tell Jordan was trying not to smile, but a big, doofy grin spread across his face.

"Um, Jordan, Brynn told me she told you that—"

"—that she just liked me as a friend," Jordan finished for her. He nodded. "Turned out that she said that because she didn't want to get in the middle of whatever was happening between us. She liiiikes me."

"Whoa. I'm—I'm shocked. She is so much nicer than I am!" Priya exclaimed. She was going to have to find something super cool to do for Brynn. The girl knew how to be a true, true friend.

"Not hard to be nicer than you," Jordan said with a grin. He gave the basketball a bounce. "Oh, yeah. She likes me. She thinks I'm fun-ny. She really likes me."

"Does she like the way you brag?" Priya asked, using two fingers to flick the ball away from him.

"It's one of her favorite things." Jordan got the ball back and spun it on his finger. "Listen, I feel like saying this is a very bad idea, but you know Spence?"

"Spence? As in Spence who we play cards with practically every night?" Priya shook her head. "Of course I know him."

"Well, he wants to hang with you after dinner during free time," Jordan said.

"We can still play cards if you and Brynn want to do something different," Priya told him. "We will manage to survive without your presence and your freaky food phobias."

Jordan lightly bounced the ball off her forehead. "No, moron. He wants to do something just the two of you. Cause he liiiikes you."

"Are you messing with me?" Priya demanded. "This is payback, isn't it?"

"I'm not mean the way you are," Jordan told her, stopping the rolling ball with his foot. "So, what should I tell him?"

"Spence is a cool guy. It could be fun. So tell him . . . tell him yes." Priya said. "Except saying that makes me feel a little nauseated. I hope he doesn't expect me to be some sort of girly girl. I know I was sort of girly on the cruise, but I'm not always like that."

"Take it from me," Jordan advised. "All you have to do is be you."

Priya thought she could handle that.

Turn the page for a sneak preview of

# camp
# CONFIDENTIAL

## OVER & OUT

*available soon!*

chapter

Hey Matt (aka Einstein wannabe),

How's it going, Dr. Bloomenstein? I
can't believe Mom let you set up a mini–
science lab in the basement. That's a scary
thought. With all those test tubes you've
got, you could be creating radioactive
cockroaches down there or something. Just
be sure to let them loose in Adam's room,
not mine, k?

I can't believe there're only two
weeks left here at camp. The summer's
gone by way too fast. It's such a downer to

think about leaving. But I'm still planning on getting in as much fun as possible while I'm here. No, Big Bro, before you start with one of your lectures, this doesn't mean pranks. Since I got in trouble with Dr. Steve last summer for all my pranking (the animal-shack fiasco in particular), I'm breaking new records for good behavior (even without Stephanie around to play the "Third Parent"... ha-ha). I only raided Adam's cabin once so far—talk about exhibiting amazing self-control. Besides, I've got way more important things to worry about right now.

Color War starts next week, and I've been putting in some serious preparation time on the soccer field and basketball court. Remember how I was voted MVP for the Blue team last year? It'll be tough to top that, but I'm gonna try! Alex and I have been scrimmaging on the soccer field in all of our free time. She's even better than last year, Matt! I really hope we're on the same color team again this year. If we are, we might be able to bring home a Lakeview Champion title. Even though we're in different cabins (which was a major bummer at the beginning of the summer) we're still awesome friends like always. And we're ready to kick some big-time Color War butt!

Anyway, enjoy your—ugh—science. Just don't blow anything up unless it's Mom's spinach casserole. That I can live without. I better sign off. Natalie and Alyssa are threatening to toss my candy stash in the lake if we don't go to dinner RIGHT NOW. Yeesh. They must really be starving if they're *this excited about the mess-hall food. I'm just hoping it's not a mystery meat loaf day. I miss you, and I'll see you soon.*

*Love,*

*Jenna*

▲ ▲ ▲

Jenna Bloom looked hungrily at the platters of french fries that the CITs, or counselors-in-training, were marching through the mess hall.

"Are you seriously going to eat those?" her friend Alex asked.

"Yup." Jenna grinned. "They're the only things that look edible." She and Alex had to eat at separate tables with their different bunks, but they always had a few minutes to chat beforehand. She saw Alex sizing up a tray of mac and cheese. "Don't tell me that you're going to eat *that*? It looks a little curdly, if you ask me."

"It doesn't look that bad," Alex said. "But then again, I have to think positive about it, since I'm sick of french fries and this is the only other thing I can eat. Besides the mushy broccoli."

"Sorry about that," Jenna said. "But you're probably way healthier than any of the rest of us, especially me." She knew from their last summer together that Alex had juvenile diabetes and had to be really careful about what she ate. Pasta and vegetables were good for her, but some other kinds of food, especially ones full of sugar, were dangerous for her to eat. But now that all the girls knew about Alex's condition, they were careful to be understanding of it. Jenna grinned and elbowed her playfully. "And if it makes you feel better, I asked my mom to send some honey cookies in the last box of goodies she mailed me. Just for you. The package came this morning, and it's sitting under my bunk . . . right now. I figured we'd both need some extra energy to perfect our soccer skills for Color War," Jenna said. "Hey, what did you request for your final electives?"

"I asked for sports and photography," Alex said as they headed toward their tables.

"Photography?" Jenna asked. "I didn't know you were into taking pictures."

Alex blushed. "Well, I—I've been wanting to learn the right way to use my camera for a while now, and . . . and . . ." She stammered, and the words died away.

"And you wanted to be in an elective with Adam?" Jenna teased, watching Alex's cheeks flush bubblegum pink. She rolled her eyes. Adam, Jenna's brother, was the camp's best photographer. Last summer, Alex had had a tiny crush on Adam, and every once in a while Jenna still caught Alex looking at Adam with a shy smile on her face. But there was no way Alex could possibly *really* like Adam Spasm again, was there?

Alex giggled. "I don't know. I might not even get to be in photography. What electives did you ask for?"

"I asked for sports, too, of course," Jenna said. "If we both get sports, we can practice soccer and basketball every day. Man, if we're on the same color team, we'll be unstoppable!"

"Lakeview legends, reigning victorious," Alex said. "I can't wait."

"We'll go down in history, that's for sure," Jenna said, slapping her a high five before they split up to sit down at their separate bunk tables. She and Alex had been coming to Camp Lakeview for the past five years, and it seemed like they'd been friends forever. They'd always been in the same bunk together, until this summer. This summer, all of the girls from last year's bunk 3C had been divided into separate bunks. Jenna was in 4A, and Alex was in 4C. But that hadn't stopped the two of them from staying close friends. Sports were what Jenna and Alex did best, and Jenna couldn't wait to spend as much of her free time with Alex on the soccer field as possible.

Jenna plopped down at 4A's table next to Natalie and Tori, who were in the middle of a debate about Tad Maxwell's latest hairstyle for his new movie, *Spy in the Sahara*. Tad was a huge movie star, but he was also Natalie's dad. He'd shown up at camp once last summer and had practically caused a fainting frenzy of mass proportion among the girls. But for the most part, Nat liked to keep a low profile about him. Except, apparently, today.

"I can't believe he got hair extensions for this movie," Nat said, shaking her head as she looked at Tad's photo in the issue of *Star Scoop* that Tori had brought with her to lunch. "His hair's longer than mine now! And he's middle-aged *and* a parent. That's just not right."

"Maybe the directors wanted him to look younger," Alyssa offered, leaning over the table to inspect the photo. "It's gotta be tough to be over forty and competing with guys like Orlando Bloom for roles. Hollywood isn't very forgiving of wrinkles."

"Well, I think he looks cute," Tori said. "He has to look rugged if he's roughing it on a camel in the desert for this movie."

Nat groaned, her head in her hands. "If anyone else calls my dad 'cute' again, I'm in serious danger of losing my lunch."

"If it makes you feel better, I don't think he's cute," Jenna jumped in. "And I think he looks better with a buzz cut."

"Thank you!" Nat said, snapping the magazine shut.

"No problem." Jenna smiled as she dipped a couple of her french fries in ketchup.

She was just about to pop them into her mouth when Alyssa's eyes widened in horror. "Jenna, stop!"

Jenna froze. "What?" she asked, glancing down at her food. But then she saw it. The charred clump of . . . what? A bug? A piece of yesterday's mystery meat loaf? Jenna couldn't tell for sure. But whatever it was, it was stuck to the side of one of the fries looking *very* unappetizing. "Eeeuw!" she cried, flinging the fry back onto her plate in disgust. "How gross is that?" She dumped her fries in the trash and dug into her chicken fingers instead, but only after carefully inspecting them to make sure they were free of UFOs (Unidentified Food Objects) first. "Okay, guys. Word to the wise. Avoid the french fries at all costs."

Just then, Tori gave a low whistle.

"Hottie," she whispered excitedly, "twelve o'clock. Headed this way."

Jenna looked up to see Adam walking toward their table. "Gross, Tori," she said. "My brother is *so* not hot. That's a totally disturbing picture."

"Not Adam," Nat said. "I think Tori means the guy *with* Adam. Who is *he?*"

The stranger walking with Adam hadn't even registered on Jenna's radar before, but now she took a second look as they came closer. Even Jenna had to admit that the blond-haired, blue-eyed guy looked more like a boarding-school preppy than a camper. From the sleek sunglasses perched on his head to his boating shoes and polo shirt, he was primped, polished, and could've been straight out of one of those *Star Scoop* photos.

"No way," Tori whispered. "Those *cannot* be Hugo Boss sunglasses he's wearing."

"Hugo who?" Jenna asked.

"It's a store so expensive that even my dad refuses to shop there," Nat said. "He thinks it's way overpriced."

"And for your dad the super spy," Alyssa added, "that's saying a lot."

Adam stopped at their table and ruffled Jenna's brown hair before she could stop him. She gave him a shove in return.

"Hey, guys, Dr. Steve asked me to introduce his nephew to everyone here today," Adam explained, nodding to the guy at his side. "This is Blake Wetherly. He's from East Hampton in New York. He's visiting for the last two weeks of camp, and he's bunking with us in 4E."

"Hello, ladies," Blake said after Adam had introduced all the girls. He flashed a brilliant grin worthy of a young Brad Pitt. "Nice to meet you all."

"You too," Nat, Tori, Chelsea, and Karen all echoed at once.

Jenna nearly choked on a chicken finger as she looked around the table to see nearly everyone's eyelashes batting in unison at Blake. What was wrong in the world these days, when her friends went off the deep end for a guy wearing a pair of overpriced sunglasses? She sighed.

"I'm going to show Blake the ropes today," Adam explained, "and hopefully he'll get the hang of camp in enough time to get totally prepped for Color War next week, too."

"Color War? But, but," Jenna stuttered. "Dr. Steve never lets anyone participate in Color War unless they've been a camper all summer long." She looked at Blake. "Why didn't you come to camp with everyone else at the beginning of the summer?"

"I was abroad for the last month," Blake said nonchalantly, as if traveling internationally was something he did all the time. Which, Jenna suddenly realized, he probably did. "My parents have a summer house in Lake Como, Italy. We go there every year."

"How amazing! Last summer my parents took me to Paris," Tori chirped, tossing her glossy hair over her shoulder and smiling. "But I've never been to Lake Como. I'd love to hear all about it."

"Sure thing," Blake said. "But I'm starving. My dad's jet landed late. We flew here straight from Rome, and I haven't eaten since this morning. And then the limo got lost on the way here."

"Poor baby," Jenna muttered under her breath.

"This place is really out in the sticks," Blake continued. "My uncle's such a hick. You might be a redneck if you live in a place where the mosquitoes outnumber the people." He laughed as if he'd just told the funniest joke in the world, and Tori, Nat, and Karen laughed right along with him.

"Dr. Steve's great," Jenna said with a touch of defensiveness. The way Blake had said the word *hick* made it sound like a fate worse than death, and his attitude suddenly irked Jenna, who loved coming here every year, mosquitoes and all.

"And the bugs aren't too bad," Nat piped up. "I got eaten alive the first week I was here last year, but insect repellent works miracles."

"And reeks, too." Blake crinkled his nose up in

distaste. "So, is any of the grub decent around here, or should I break out the Pepto-Bismol?"

Jenna resisted the urge to tell Blake to go jump in the lake and gave him a big grin instead. "Give the french fries a try. They're super-yummy."

"Thanks," Blake said, flashing his gleaming smile again. "I'll catch you guys later at the campfire."

"What a snob!" Jenna exclaimed after Blake walked away with Adam. "If his nose were stuck up any higher in the air, he'd have altitude sickness."

Alyssa laughed. "He did seem a little full of himself."

"Maybe he just feels awkward because he doesn't know anyone here," Karen offered. "It's gotta be tough to come into camp right at the end of the summer like this."

"Not that tough," Jenna countered. "In fact, I'm guessing Blake hasn't had too many tough times in his life. His dad has a private jet, and a limo to boot? Come on."

"And he lives in the Hamptons," Tori said, whispering the word as if it were too special to say out loud. "My parents have been there before to visit some friends. My mom told me they stayed in a house with twelve bathrooms! Can you imagine?"

"I can. I'd never have to fight Stephanie for the bathroom mirror again," Jenna said dreamily, thinking of her big sister's hour-long primping sessions.

"I didn't know you ever looked in the mirror,

Jen," Chelsea quipped. "Not with that hair."

Jenna chose to ignore that remark. Chelsea was always saying something snippy, and everyone in the two bunks had learned to take her harsh words with a grain of salt.

"Doesn't Donald Trump have a mansion in the Hamptons?" Karen asked, trying to move past Chelsea's comment.

"Donald Trump has mansions everywhere," Nat replied, and snuck another look at Blake. "He is cute. But not as cute as Simon, of course."

Nat and Simon were one of the camp's couples, and they'd liked each other since last summer. But Nat was still carrying on the eternal debate of whether or not to actually kiss Simon on the lips. Jenna couldn't imagine getting anywhere near a guy's lips. No way.

Nat lifted the collar of her T-shirt up to her nose. "Does bug spray really smell that bad?"

"*Nat.*" Jenna groaned. "You do *not* smell. And if Blake wants to be all stuck-up about wearing insect repellent, let him be. He'll be covered in bites by tomorrow morning." She giggled at the thought. "And if you guys had brothers as annoying as Adam, you wouldn't think *any* guy was cute."

Jenna sighed. Guys were okay . . . some of the time, but she wasn't entirely sure she wanted to get bitten by the *lurve* bug anytime soon. She'd had a *tiny* crush on her brother's friend David earlier in the summer, but when it turned out he liked Sarah, she'd gotten over it pretty quickly. But Nat, Alex, and Tori were a different story—they and over half of Jenna's other friends were involved in major crushes.

Thankfully, just when Jenna was getting tired of the boy talk, Andie and Mia, the bunk's counselor and CIT, stood up from the table. "Singdown time!" Andie announced with a grin, and suddenly everyone forgot about boys, at least for the moment.

▲ ▲ ▲

Jenna wiped another sticky string of marsh-mallow off her chin and popped it into her mouth. Flopping back in the grass, she basked in the warmth of the campfire's glow.

"Mmmm." She gave her friends a goopy smile. "There's nothing better than s'mores."

"Really?" Nat said, taking a big bite out of her s'more sandwich and giggling as some chocolate dribbled down her chin. "I thought you loved brownies more."

"Brownies!" Jenna said longingly. "I love them, too. I bet I could make super s'mores with brownies instead of graham crackers."

"Jenna, is there anything you think about besides food?" Chelsea smirked.

"Right this second, no." Jenna laughed. She scooted over to where Karen and Alyssa sat singing a funny version of "The Bear Went over the Mountain" that they'd turned into "The Camper Got Lost on the Mountain." She threw one arm around each girl and joined in, singing the words at the top of her lungs. Soon, the three girls were hiccuping with laughter in between verses. They'd finished the singdown a while ago, but everyone in the division was still in singing mode, making up silly lyrics to songs and belting them out as the fire crackled. A couple of the counselors were writing down lyrics to the songs the bunks were making up, planning to use them for Color War later on.

"Does everyone always sing off-key around here?" a voice said behind them, and Jenna turned to see Blake standing next to Adam and Simon and wearing a look of slight annoyance on his face.

Karen saw him at the same time and froze mid-stanza, gave a little shriek of embarrassment, and dove for a marshmallow to hide her reddening cheeks.

"We sing however we want to," Alyssa said with a shrug.

Jenna smiled at that. Leave it to Alyssa to say whatever was on her mind. Jenna had always liked that about her, and she was relieved to see that Blake hadn't cast his spell on everyone . . . yet.

"That's the great thing about camp," Jenna said. "Nobody cares how bad we sound when we sing."

"Until now," Blake said, then broke into his easy smile, so that no one could be entirely sure whether he was insulting them or just kidding around.

"Wait until the final banquet," Nat said. "The whole camp sings the Lakeview Camp alma mater so loud that the windows in the mess hall rattle."

Blake yawned indifferently. "Yeah, well, we'll see

if I'm still around for the final banquet."

"What do you mean?" Tori asked. *Everybody* goes to the final banquet. This year will be my first banquet ever, and I can't wait."

"Yeah," Adam said to Blake. "You'd miss out on all the great food and fun if you didn't go. Besides, the longer you stick around camp, the better chance you have of seeing some of Jenna's pranks."

"Pranks?" Blake repeated.

"Last year Jenna let all the animals out of the nature shack and into the mess hall at the camp dance," Adam explained. "She's the master prankster in these parts."

"*Retired* master prankster," Jenna corrected. "No more big pranks for me, not after Dr. Steve threatened to kick me out of camp."

"That's *so* my uncle." Blake rolled his eyes. "He just doesn't know how to have a good time. Which is why I'm giving this camp thing a trial run before I decide whether I want to stick around or not. I can call my dad's driver to come pick me up whenever I feel like it."

Jenna rolled her eyes and leaned over to whisper to Nat. "How about he calls that driver right now?"

Just then, Simon walked over to Nat. "Is this seat taken?" he asked her.

Nat giggled. "It is now," she said, taking his hand as he sat down beside her.

Jenna sighed, scooting over to make more room for him. If Nat got any more cuddly with Simon, Jenna was going to lose her appetite. So she grabbed another marshmallow while she still had it.

Even though Nat was too lost in her own world to notice it, the next half hour just confirmed for Jenna what she already thought was true. Blake sat down with Adam near Alex and Brynn, but he refused to roast any marshmallows or sing any songs. When Brynn told a spooky ghost story that gave Jenna chills and made her huddle closer to Alyssa and Perry, Blake just rolled his eyes.

"That was lame," he snorted, standing up from the fire. "I hate to break up the party, but I'm going to find my uncle and see if I can head back to the bunk. It's, like, two o'clock in the morning in Italy right now. I'm still on Lake Como time."

"You need to find Kenny, our counselor, first," Adam told him. "He needs to know where we are at all times."

"Nah." Blake shrugged. "Uncle Steve's right over there," he pointed to where Dr. Steve was helping supervise some of the younger campers roasting marshmallows. "He'll let me leave. No problem."

"Nothing like a little favoritism," Jenna said, watching as Blake talked to Dr. Steve and then wandered off toward the bunk alone. She couldn't believe Blake was getting special treatment from Dr. Steve, but at least he was gone for the night. That was a relief.

As counselors started ushering campers off to the bunks, Jenna grinned at her friends. "Hey, I've got a fresh candy stash back in the bunk, if anyone's interested."

"You just ate five s'mores!" Chelsea gasped.

"Exactly." Jenna patted her stomach. "That leaves room for at least two of my mom's home-made brownies."

"Count me in!" Nat said.

"Me too!" Alyssa added.

"Will you allow a couple campers from the bunk next door to crash the party?" Alex asked as she walked over with Brynn and Grace.

"As long as no one mentions boys for the rest of the night," Jenna said with a smile.

"Deal!" Alex said, and the rest of the girls chimed in.

"And as long as Andie and Mia say it's okay," Jenna added. She looked at Mia and Andie expectantly, hoping they'd say yes.

"Give us a sec," Andie said, motioning Becky, the counselor from 4C, over. The three girls talked, and then all nodded in agreement. "You guys can hang out in our bunk for a while, but you'll have to wait for a half hour before you come over," Andie said. "Because we're all assigning final electives now."

Alex and Brynn squealed with excitement, and Grace grinned. "That's worth waiting for," she said. "Besides, the casting list just got posted for the camp play. Becky said we could check it out before we go to the bunk. We're doing *Into the Woods* this year."

At the end of every summer, a big drama production was put on for all the campers on the night of the final banquet. Last year, the play had been *Peter Pan*, and Grace had played the best Wendy that Jenna had ever seen. Grace and Brynn both loved acting, and they were really great at it, too.

"I've never seen that play before," Jenna said.

Nat clapped her hands. "It's not a play. It's a musical, and I *love* it! It's the one that has all the fairy tales rolled into one show. That was one of the first shows my parents took me to see on Broadway." Nat and Tori were both in drama with Brynn and Grace, but Nat had decided not to audition for the show this year because, she said, she preferred acting serious drama parts instead of musicals.

"And I saw it when it came to L.A.," Tori said. She'd auditioned for the part of Little Red Riding Hood, and she was practically jumping up and down with excitement now, too. She turned to Andie. "Oh, Andie, can I please go look with them?"

Andie laughed. "Sure. Just be quick, okay?" she said, but Tori was already racing away with Grace and Brynn.

"So, I'll see you after we get our electives," Alex said to Jenna, heading toward her bunk. "Wish me good luck so I'll get sports."

"Good luck," Jenna called out. "To both of us!"

She waved good-bye, making a silent wish as she walked back to her own bunk that she and Alex would both get the electives they'd asked for.

Once everyone got settled back at the bunk and Tori reappeared, breathlessly exclaiming that she'd gotten the part of Little Red Riding Hood in the play, Andie took out her clipboard for the final elective assignments. Jenna and the other girls all rushed over to Andie, hovering over her to view their assignments.

"I won't be able to give them out if you suffocate me first!" Andie laughed, but the girls were already looking for their names on the clipboard.

"Sports and boating," Jenna cried when she saw the electives next to her name. "Yes!"

"Are you ready to take on nature again?" Alyssa teased Nat as she looked at the clipboard.

"Not yet. I think I need until next year to mentally prepare myself for that," Nat said. Last year, Nat had nature as one of her first electives, but everyone knew that the closest she wanted to get to nature was painting her nails by the lake under a tree. "I got newspaper and drama."

"Um, Andie?" Tori asked hesitantly. "I know I already requested drama and art, but, um, do you happen to know what electives Blake signed up for? I thought maybe I'd be able to switch mine."

Andie shook her head. "Sorry, Tori. I don't think Blake's been given anything yet. Dr. Steve wanted to see how many empty spots were left in each elective before deciding where he might fit in."

"Oh." Tori's face fell, but then she brightened.

"That's okay. Maybe he'll end up in my art class anyway."

"If he does, he probably won't want to touch the paints for fear of getting his Hugo Boss glasses dirty," Jenna said.

Just then, there was knock on the door, and Alex stuck her head around it. "Can we come in?"

"Yup," Andie said. "We just finished with electives."

"Us too!" Alex said, coming in with Brynn and Grace.

Jenna caught Alex's eye, and Alex gave her a thumbs-up sign and a big smile. That was all Jenna needed. She knew they had both gotten their first choice, and now they could play sports together for an extra hour every day.

"We have more big news," Brynn said with a grin after the girls had finished talking about who got what electives. "Grace and I got our parts for *Into the Woods*."

"And?" Nat asked expectantly.

Grace beamed. "I'm Cinderella."

"And I'm the witch!" Brynn said, raising her hands like claws and hissing in a villainous way.

"Congrats!" Jenna said. "You guys both get extra brownies and so does Tori, aka Little Red. The chocolate will help you all remember your lines."

"What?" Chelsea cried. "Since when does chocolate improve your memory?"

Jenna grinned. "As far as I know, there's not much that chocolate doesn't improve," she said, making everyone laugh.

As Jenna dug into her candy stash, she smiled and promised herself that nothing was ever going to distract her from her friends or from the soccer field and basketball court—particularly not some fancy schmancy guy from the Hamptons. Camp was almost over, and she was going to make the rest of her time here unforgettable.